**When she sat, words poured out of Cole of their own volition.**

"You haven't said too much, Lindsay. What you said was probably one of the nicest things anyone has ever said to me. And you have my word, I absolutely will not read more than friendship into any time we mutually decide to spend together."

When Lillie laid her head on Lindsay's knee, Cole might have smiled, if not for the seriousness of the conversation he wasn't done having. "Because as out of character as it is for me, I find myself thinking it feels right to spend time with you, too."

Her glance was long and intrusive. He had no problem whatsoever withstanding it.

"You're my boss."

"Only at work," he told her. "And not really, because you're contracted help. You're your boss. I'm—or rather, Elite Paper is—your client. That aside, though, in a town the size of this one, if outside the workplace people couldn't associate on a personal level with people with whom they worked, then... we'd all have to walk around ignoring one another."

Her grin lit up her face. And his spirits.

"Then I'm glad we're in a small town," she told him.

Dear Reader,

I'm so glad you picked up this book! The story is what I like to read—meaty and emotional, with no easy answers and love that knows no boundaries.

And there are two very special extras about this one. First, while it's a Sierra's Web book, it's set in Shelter Valley, Arizona—a town I created twenty years ago writing for Harlequin Superromance. If you like the characters here, you've got fifteen other stories you can read that will keep you in a place where people reach out to each other, welcome strangers and always give second chances.

The other extra here is Lillie. She's an old dog. A rescue and service dog. Mostly, she tunes in to people and tries to offer strength and support when they're emotionally distressed. Lillie reminds me of a dog I used to have. She's in a canine body with human understanding. Or so it seems. She just has to look at you for you to see inside yourself and discover the truths waiting there. Old dog, new truth. She's also fine with offering her fur to help soak up your tears. Or a lick on the cheek to help celebrate your joy.

So read on... If I didn't get it right, Lillie will!

*TTQ*

# Old Dogs, New Truths

---

## TARA TAYLOR QUINN

HARLEQUIN
**SPECIAL**
EDITION

ISBN-13: 978-1-335-59416-7

Old Dogs, New Truths

Harlequin Enterprises ULC
22 Adelaide St. West, 41st Floor
Toronto, Ontario M5H 4E3, Canada
www.Harlequin.com

**Printed in U.S.A.**

Recycling programs
for this product may
not exist in your area.

A *USA TODAY* bestselling author of over 105 novels in twenty languages, **Tara Taylor Quinn** has sold more than seven million copies. Known for her intense emotional fiction, Ms. Quinn's novels have received critical acclaim in the UK and most recently from Harvard. She is the recipient of the Readers' Choice Award and has appeared often on local and national TV, including *CBS Sunday Morning*.

For TTQ offers, news and contests, visit www.tarataylorquinn.com!

### Books by Tara Taylor Quinn

**Harlequin Special Edition**

***Shelter Valley Stories***

*Their Secret Twins*

***Sierra's Web***

*His Lost and Found Family*
*Reluctant Roommates*
*Her Best Friend's Baby*

***Furever Yours***

*Love off the Leash*

***The Parent Portal***

*A Baby Affair*
*Her Motherhood Wish*
*A Mother's Secrets*
*The Child Who Changed Them*
*Their Second-Chance Baby*
*Her Christmas Future*

Visit the Author Profile page
at Harlequin.com for more titles.

To my Annie girl, Lillie's look-alike. For Taylor Marie—my most faithful companion for seventeen years. And for LeeLee Marie, who grabbed Taylor's torch and is forging her own way of blessing my life. I hope and pray that what I had/have to offer you was/is enough. You three all have my forever love.

## Chapter One

"We're set to go?" Lindsay Warren-Smythe, heiress and charity chief fundraising officer—aka Lindsay Warren, bohemian artist—couldn't help the nervous smile that trembled on her lips. Nor the jump in her heart rate as her friend of many years, Sierra's Web expert lawyer Savannah Compton, met her look with a compassionate gaze—and a nod.

Seated at a secluded table on the outdoor terrace of a private club overlooking a meticulously maintained golf course, the Phoenix valley and the gorgeous mountains beyond, Savannah slid a manila envelope across the expanse between them. "It's all there.

"The apartment is being rented through your Lindsay Warren, LLC." Savannah's words twisted the knot further in Lindsay's stomach. "It's small, one bedroom, outdoor entrance, second floor so you'll have to walk up a set of cement stairs to get to it. Your key's in there."

Lindsay looked at the big bulky envelope. Didn't touch it.

"You submitted a job application at Elite Paper using your Lindsay Warren email, with a link to your website and online shop, and have an interview at the home office in Shelter Valley this afternoon. Your apartment's about a mile from the office. Elite Paper has the entire second floor of a building adjacent to the university. The town itself is small, an hour or so drive from here."

Listening, absorbing every word, Lindsay couldn't slow the flutters in her stomach.

"We purchased an old, but clean, sedan for you. It's light yellow to fit Lindsay Warren's nature. Has a handmade Navajo dream catcher hanging from the rearview mirror. It's parked outside, back of the lot, west corner. The keys are in there." Without breaking eye contact, Savannah nodded toward the envelope on the table.

Almost as though she knew that if she looked away, Lindsay would get up and run.

She could leave anytime. She was a free agent.

A wealthy free agent.

If money counted as wealth.

Savannah and her partners at Sierra's Web were officially working for Lindsay. At Lindsay's expense.

The reminder did nothing to calm her nerves.

"You'll be meeting with Chief of Personnel Cole Bennet this afternoon. He's a big guy, six-three, red hair. Nice man."

Yada, yada, yada. Cole Bennet was a means to an end. He could be a total jerk as long as he gave her the job.

Odd though, that the head of Elite Paper had hired what sounded like a bodyguard type for an employee relations position. Was that because one had something to hide? And needed protection in every aspect of his life? Watching his back?

Fit the profile of a guy hiding from a previous life.

"You sure you want to do this?" Savannah's soft, warm tone lost all professionalism, her brown eyes pools of compassion. "We can make all of this disappear as easily as we set it up," she continued.

Lindsay didn't shake her head.

She didn't nod, either.

Her offhand, half joke to Savannah, months before at a charitable function Lindsay had been hosting, had snowballed and was changing her entire life.

Even if she gave back the envelope and retreated to her lovely home on the beach in La Jolla.

She'd never thought Sierra's Web would actually find her father. Or, if they had, the irresponsible, heartless louse would be either in prison or dead.

He wouldn't be the owner of a company that was known for the artistic quality of the greeting cards, card stock and wrapping papers they produced.

The job she'd be interviewing for was one she'd have jumped at when she'd graduated college. Right up her alley.

If not for the grandparents who'd raised her.

They forbade any hint of her bohemian artist soul to emerge into the air.

"You change your mind?" Savannah's gentle question held no judgment.

"I've got a great life," she said then, looking her friend of five years in the eye. "I'm really good at what I do…"

"The best," Savannah told her. "Sierra's Web would love to have you on staff."

"I'm keeping several really important California-based national charities afloat," she said, more for her own edification than in response to the expert lawyer. "I love that I can do that."

Savannah's nod was accompanied by a smile as she said, "I know." An open-ended offer to Lindsay to work at Sierra's Web had come at the close of the first job Sierra's Web had done for Lindsay. Savannah had successfully defended Amanda's Army—an LA-based charity that donated to children's hospitals—from a tax fraud charge that had been wrongfully brought. Lindsay's fundraising skills had been under excruciating investigation not only by the prosecutor, but by Sierra's Web experts as well. In the end, she'd come out as completely compliant with the law, innovative and highly gifted at her job. Savannah had talked about charities all over the country that could benefit from her efforts.

Problem was, she was still Grace and William Warren-Smythe's only living offspring, and a grandchild at that. She'd been raised with an intense sense of obligation to the city and state, and to the people who'd raised her.

Her grandparents were fond of Savannah. On more than one occasion, they had hired Winchester Holmes, the Sierra's Web finance expert, to oversee particularly complicated investments. But they'd never ever, in a million lifetimes, approve of Lindsay deserting her full-time work for carefully chosen charities to pop in and out of hundreds all over the country. And the manila envelope on that table—would devastate them.

As would the work Sierra's Web had done to put it there.

"You want to know what we found out about him? Other than that he's the owner of Elite Paper Company and lives in Shelter Valley, Arizona?"

Lindsay had yet to give a yay or nay to Savannah's previous question, about going ahead or nixing the whole plan.

And her friend, expert lawyer that she was, was giving Lindsay a nudge to get to the answer. She'd seen Savannah in action enough to know that much.

Lindsay played along, nodding. She wouldn't be in Phoenix, sitting at that table, if there wasn't a need deep inside, driving her.

"He's married. Has been for twenty-five years, to the same woman. They have three kids. Two boys and a girl, ranging in age from eleven to fifteen."

At least he'd married one woman he'd knocked up.

She had three half siblings!

Nice of him to give them his legitimacy. His time.

Two brothers and a sister!

Who'd grown up with a father.

Thoughts chased over themselves, nobody winning.

"The public financials of Elite Paper are impressive," Savannah dropped into the middle of Lindsay's silent war. "Winchester's report is in there, but he said to tell you that Brent Wilson appears to be a man who puts quality over making money. He could easily be a billionaire, but spends so much on high-end machinery and materials, on employee benefits, that he's only worth millions. Since Elite Paper is a privately held company, he can get away with it."

Brent Wilson.

The man who'd fathered her.

And then abandoned her mother. Driving the woman to seek solace from her broken heart in the form of the fancy, expensive and very illegal drugs that had killed her...

"You said you never got the whole truth about what happened between your mom and dad..." Savannah's soft words floated on the artificially cooled air blowing from discreetly set air conditioners in the guise of planters around them.

"My mother died of an overdose before my first birthday. And you know Mimi and Papa. They think it's a futile course of action to dwell on the past. Other than regaling me with every picture, every memory of her they had before she met my father, of course."

Poor little rich girl. The image popped up to taunt her. Sitting outside in hundred-degree heat, blissfully cool, surrounded by hanging, gloriously colorful plants on an elegant balcony that overlooked one of the nation's most beautiful cities.

As Savannah motioned for refills of the prickly pear iced tea they'd both ordered, Lindsay picked up the envelope in front of her. Pulled a pen out of the big colorful cloth shoulder bag she'd purchased a few years back, but only carried on those rare occasions when she was far away from home, attending a gathering as Lindsay Warren.

Before she realized what she was doing, she had a broken heart—half darkened, half outline only—drawn with shading and raw edges, taking up the center of the envelope.

"You're a fantastic businesswoman, Lins. A wonderful, attentive granddaughter, a loyal friend to so many. And look at you. Half of your heart is dark."

Savannah's words, barely above a whisper, hit her like a tsunami. She jerked back. Looked at her drawing, and then up at her friend.

"Think of how much more you'd have to give to them all if you could live with full lights shining."

She nodded.

Acknowledged to herself that she'd been stalling because she hadn't been able to back out. Savannah's closing argument had given the Warren-Smythe part of her permission to pick up that envelope. Open it.

And take out the keys to the rest of her life.

"Seriously, Nicky? You and Josh want me to be his godfather? What about Dane?" Sitting in his second-story, fully windowed corner office, Cole Bennet stared at the perimeter of elegant mountains surrounding Shelter Valley, grinning from ear to ear, even as he named Josh's best friend.

"Josh says he wants you, too. His sister is going to be godmother." And he got it. He was Nicky's pick. Her best friend.

Also, her ex-fiancé, but that was all in the past.

While leaving him at the altar hadn't been her best move, he'd grown to understand how right she'd been to call off the wedding. She'd loved him so much she hadn't wanted to lose him, but couldn't bring herself to tell him that she hadn't been in love with him.

The story of his big, extra ten pounds overweight, red-headed life.

But he'd learned over the years, most particularly when he'd been so genuinely happy for his friend at her wedding, that while he adored her, he hadn't been in love with her, either.

He'd been thrilled to have a real girlfriend. To have the prospect of a wife—and a family down the road. He'd loved Nicky as a friend.

Still did.

Just as he was already half in love with the kid she was carrying. "Then, of course, I'm his godfather," he said, still smiling. "I'm going to teach that kid how to be friends with women," he said. "Real friends, not just as a way to get in their pants."

Her burst of laughter made him chuckle, too.

"You might want to wait a year or two before introducing the whole birds and bees thing," she said, and gave him the rundown from her most recent doctor's appointment. Still with three months to go, Nicky was reveling in every moment of the event she'd been waiting for her entire life. While some of the details blurred on him a bit, he was happy to hear her happiness.

And would have listened to her gab on endlessly, if not for the upcoming appointment staring at him from the daily event calendar his assistant had placed on his desk first thing that morning.

Lindsay Warren. Visual Artist. Whose work included pieces using dried flowers instead of paint to create landscapes. Jewelry pieces she made herself. Original paintings—mostly of flowers in random places, like growing between the cracks in a sidewalk.

And exquisite greeting cards.

The latter had his attention.

He'd already been all over her shop on one of the top artisan-selling apps.

Everything shipped from California.

He'd need her to relocate. Couldn't imagine, with her talent, inventory and Southern California address, she'd have any desire to do so. Their job listing had been for a contracted position, not an actual employee, but the position was full-time and had to be in-house. She'd have to give up a lot of her own work.

Those were the things keeping her off the top of his list. While Elite Paper would benefit greatly from her level of ability and experience, he'd all but decided on hiring the young man he'd seen the day before, a Montford University graduate. With the small but elite university being right there in town, Victor had already done a residency with Elite and could start immediately. Cole just had this one last interview to get through before finalizing the deal.

His conversation with Nicky still filling him with smiles, he was ready when Ms. Lindsay Warren was shown into his office.

And immediately sobered. In her long black skirt—

made out of what looked like thin T-shirt material—with a black-and-white lace and tie-dyed flowing tank-style top and three-inch-high flip-flops with lots of silver glitz on the straps, she was…stunning.

The long blond hair that flowed around her shoulders, the perfectly shaped body and smiling lips beneath big brown eyes…

He was on overload.

For a geeky-looking guy like him, it might have been a standard reaction, but Cole had spent his life around beautiful women. Nicky had won a swimsuit modeling contract right out of high school. Beautiful women gravitated to him for support when their boyfriends or lovers behaved in ways that were insensitive, that hurt them. Looking to him for male insight. And a way to help make situations better.

Lucky for both him and them, he generally could.

"Is something wrong?" Her voice was like a melody, and Cole stood.

Felt his body towering over her, his slight paunch visible above the leather belt keeping his dress pants in place. He adjusted his tie, using it to cover the distention. And sat back down.

"Lindsay?" he asked, stupidly as it turned out, since she'd already been announced.

"Yes, I'm sorry I'm early—I just… I really want this job." She was nervous.

Immensely so.

Which brought Cole back from whatever weird universe her arrival had plopped him in. "No worries," he told her. "I was just going over your file. It's more than impressive." He knew how to put people at ease.

With complete sincerity. Nothing he'd have to walk back later.

The combination served him well. At work. And in life.

Just noticing the portfolio she'd carried in with her as she pulled it up to open it on the back of an armchair, he invited her to have a seat. To use his desk. Smiled at her. "I'm eager to see your work," he told her, leaning forward to help her balance the portfolio as she unzipped it. "Even virtually I can tell it pops."

So much so, he'd wanted to meet her. Even knowing that he probably wasn't going to be able to hire her. The open position had come available with no warning right before delivery dates for holiday material. Meaning he had to fill it immediately. He had no time for relocation to happen, even if she agreed to the position once she knew the details.

He'd been most intrigued by her landscapes entirely "painted" with dried florals, but knew there'd be no reason for her to have loaded those up in that leather binding for him to see. Were he a museum curator, and art show arranger, then certainly, but...

"Oh, these are fantastic," he blurted, breaking into his own thoughts as he picked up the two greeting cards she'd laid down first. Both depicting Christmas trees—made completely out of dried florals. He asked if he could take a photo of them, to show Brent Wilson, the owner of Elite Paper Company.

"I know that Elite doesn't have the capacity to use

this medium, but you could get the same effect with the resins you already use. I know Elite uses plant-based, not synthetic," she added, after giving him permission to photograph her work. And then, sitting in the chair across from his desk—on the edge of the chair—she chewed on her bottom lip, glancing from the total of ten cards, in various paint and pen mediums, she'd laid out before him. Then looking up at his face, and back down.

Working for a man committed to quality first, Cole knew the best when he saw it. Was trying to wrangle a plan that would allow him to overwork a few people until she could come on board.

Which went totally against his personal, as well as company, policies. People came first.

Always.

But the nervous woman sitting across from him obviously fit that designation, too.

"The position is full-time, and requires you to work from our offices here, in the design studio located on the opposite wing of this floor."

He had to put an end to the interview before he led her on. Or made an offer he couldn't keep.

"That's fine. I've already rented a place temporarily. In case I get the job."

Was this woman for real?

"Is there any possibility you could start right away?"

"As in now? This afternoon?" She hadn't balked. At all.

The stars were aligned, as Nicky would say.

He grinned. "Tomorrow would be soon enough," he half joked at the audacity of his request. "We'd start with me taking you to tour the production plant in Phoenix in the morning, so you could get a feel for how your designs will be implemented. Then you could familiarize yourself with the art studio here. Every artist has their own space off of a central area that houses the larger design tables, cutters and walls of supply cabinets filled with glues and embellishments, for the card design part of it all. Your office comes equipped with your own smaller drawing board."

He was rambling like a schoolboy. Or felt like one.

Talking as though he'd hired her. When he'd practically given the job to someone else.

"Starting tomorrow would be great," she said then, standing as she started collecting her cards and placing them carefully back into her portfolio. "That gives me the afternoon to get moved into my apartment."

While he stood there grinning and nodding big, even for him, she named her new address. About a mile away from where they stood.

One of the town's most modest apartment complexes. Its only big complex. Filled mostly with college seniors and graduate students who no longer had dorms on campus.

"We haven't discussed terms," he told her, confused as to why she didn't seem to care about money or benefits at all. In his five years in his current position, he'd never met anyone even a little bit like this woman.

She seemed to ooze emotion, but didn't appear to care about the things that generally mattered most to the people he served. Many starving artists had found permanent, affluent homes at Elite Paper Company.

"Oh, right." Stopping with her hand on the zipper of her portfolio, she bit her bottom lip again. Clearly uncomfortable.

Which put Cole right back on track. Easing the discomfort. He named the top end of the generous salary range that had been posted for the position. Rattled off the list of benefits that came with the money. And then, having been faced before with talented people who hadn't yet been paid for their craft, he said, "If you need a retainer, we can head down to HR right now, get your paperwork done and I'll approve whatever you need, up to a two-week pay period."

"Oh!" Gathering her things quickly, she practically ran for the door. "That's okay. I'm good. I just…this was so…easy. I got the job?"

Yeah, he was definitely off his mark with her. Way off. "You got the job."

She blinked. Frowned. Then her expression flattened into blankness. "Well, good then. If you tell me how to get to HR, I'll go ahead and get that part done."

He walked her down, instead. Something he always did with new hires. But then he hung around, making excuses to do so, keeping an eye on her process at the desk in the far corner. Staying present until everything was signed and finalized.

Which was something he'd never done before.

## Chapter Two

Lindsay wasn't in the car with Cole Bennet for five minutes the next morning before she was jittery again. Guilt, she figured.

Fooled agitatedly with one of the three pairs of earrings hanging from her lobe. Worried that her colorfully tie-died spaghetti-strap dress and flip-flops, typical Lindsay Warren apparel, were wrong for a production plant tour.

More guilt?

And yet, working with Mary in HR the day before—and getting an impromptu tour of the studio space when she bumped into another artist on her way out of the building who offered to take her back and show her their area—she'd been fine. A bit excited even.

In an apprehensive sort of way.

But with Cole—as he'd told her to call him—there

was more. She'd accepted a job from him under false pretenses. Was so much more than she'd said she was.

She hadn't lied to him. But she kept looking at his hands on the steering wheel and wondering what they'd feel like threading through her hair.

Reason enough to feel remorse.

It had to be a distraction. Her way of not thinking about the fact that she'd just accepted a job with her father's company. That the man she was with knew Brent Wilson. But she pretended it was the guy's aura. The essence that he seemed to carry with him into the space he occupied. At least any space with her in it.

The guy was huge—a good nine inches taller than her. Like the bodyguard she'd initially suspected when Savannah had described him. Not someone she'd want to do wrong.

Funny how the little bit of extra weight around his waist tempered any sense of fear she might otherwise have had around him. Alone with him.

It didn't make him appear any less strong.

But his being not quite "perfect" by some women's standards made him more accessible. Endeared her to him a bit.

And, dammit, attracted her.

Because appearances aside, she wasn't perfect, either.

She'd grown up with a piece of her soul missing. One she'd yet to find. Had resigned herself to the fact that she would never find it, until she'd met Savannah. And had witnessed, firsthand, some of the miracles Sierra's Web had brought about.

As they waited at the light that would let them access the ramp to enter the highway into Phoenix, Lindsay cringed as Cole turned and caught her looking at him.

"Yes," he said, grinning. "The red is real. The curls are as tight as they look. And I don't change either because I kind of like both."

She might have thought he was self-conscious about both if not for the mastery of confidence he'd shown as he'd spoken.

"I like them, too," she told him. Deciding on the spot. The red hair, the curls, even the hint of freckles across the bridge of his nose, the rounded shape of his head—they reached out to her. Perfection in being different than the world's norms where beauty was concerned. "I'd like to draw you."

But only if she could get the sense of happiness that walked into a room with the man. Maybe not happiness, her artist's heart amended. More than happiness.

Way more than contentment. Like she was bonding with him, which was ridiculous.

The man seemed to genuinely like himself and the world he inhabited.

Which was far more than she could say about herself.

But what credibility did she have where he was concerned, really? She'd known the guy a total of an hour, adding up all the minutes they'd been in the same space together.

"Well, that's a first," he said on a chuckle as he pulled onto the freeway.

"What?"

"I've been working around artists for years. Never before had one express a desire to get my likeness down."

Her estimation of Elite Paper artists went down a notch. Still, she'd expected the day touring her father's production plant to be nothing more than disappointment.

The thought brought her to the list of questions she'd committed to memory the night before, sitting alone in a sterile, cheaply furnished living area—one in which she could see the kitchen and the bedroom from the living room couch.

She had an hour's drive to and from the city in which to find out about her father. And determine Step Three.

Step One had been finding the man.

Two had been the plan that would let her meet him, figure him out, without him knowing who she was.

Three was to either out herself to him, or get the hell out of Dodge before anyone figured out who she was.

Either way, Step Three meant getting the hell out of Dodge. She'd only taken a month's leave of absence, though she'd worked three years straight without more than a few days off at a time.

Her grandparents thought she was currently on a cruise. Releasing tension built up during an intense three years.

"Have you ever been on a cruise?" she asked her intriguing driver—and current boss—when she was supposed to be focused on obtaining daddy news.

"No."

"Yeah, me neither."

Strange. All her life she'd craved answers almost as

much as she'd wished her mother back to life and free from addiction. And there she was, with access to parts of the truth from the first person she'd met who actually knew her father, and she couldn't seem to make herself ask for it.

Afraid to find out that Brent Wilson was as much of a schmuck as she'd grown up thinking him to be? Albeit one who ran a business with quality and people more important than profit.

Or, maybe worse, to find out he was a great husband, father, employer, and she and her mother were the only ones Brent Wilson had trashed?

"You ever climb a mountain?" Cole's question, said with a twinkle of interest in the glance he sent her way, pulled her away from darker thoughts.

"No." She looked around at the towering natural majesty on all sides of them—some just haze in the distance. "Have you?"

"Yep. I've climbed to the top of one of the tallest ranges in Phoenix," he told her. "Made it by clawing my way straight up weather-smoothed rock at some points, feeling like I was all that. And then looked down." His gaze on the three lanes filled with traffic heading into Phoenix from Tucson, the next biggest town a couple of hours southeast, Cole still had a grin on his face.

She couldn't seem to get enough of looking at him. Finding his smile contagious. And she didn't even know what she was smiling about.

"I'm guessing the view was fantastic. Not to mention the high of, you know, having what it took to actually climb the mountain. A lot of us tend to think of life's hurdles as having to climb mountains." She liked the metaphor a lot. To know that you actually had the inner strength, as well as the physical endurance, to climb mountains…would mean that you'd have an awareness of your capabilities when it came to facing hard challenges.

Such as meeting the father who'd found you worthless?

"The view was great," Cole said, still wearing a bit of a grin. "Phenomenal, actually. Being on top of the world like that. It was the same view you get from an airplane, only I got up there under my own steam, not some turbofan engine…"

Right. Exactly. That.

She needed to climb a mountain.

"But that's not what I was referring to," Cole said then, getting them into the far-left carpool lane and bypassing a lot of the traffic. "I figured the tough part was climbing the mountain, right?"

She nodded.

"Yeah, then I stood up and looked down at steep, solid sheet rock and wondered how in the hell I was going to get back down. A guy my size…lots of weight to propel you downward. Too big to ride on the back of one more experienced. And too late to rethink my choice to go up."

She was smiling full out at that point—mostly because of the humor in his voice. And because she knew, since she was sitting there with him, he'd made it back just fine.

"What did you do?" She had to know.

"The only thing a big guy with brains could do. I sat on my butt, rubber-soled boots in front of me, and slid down."

Her completely unladylike guffaw of laughter, chortling up out of her depths, embarrassed her.

Until he laughed as loudly, joining her in joy.

And then, maybe for the first time in her adult life, she didn't care how she looked. Or sounded. Or how others saw her.

She just wanted to keep laughing.

Cole couldn't believe his good luck. Brent had been thrilled to hear the news of their most recent artist hire when Cole had stopped in to have dinner with him and Emily and the kids after work the night before. Not only was Lindsay Warren a gifted artist—and willing to work for their paper company—she was nice, too.

Really nice. She listened as people spoke to her. Not just him, but even the janitor in the hall the day before. And the other employees he'd seen her meet. That morning, when he'd stopped by her apartment to pick her up, she was outside chatting with an older woman who'd been out walking her dog. The woman had been smiling. And the dog wagging his tail when Lindsay bent down to tell him goodbye.

Gorgeous. And nice. The type of woman who'd gravitated to him since high school.

As opposed to those who had the looks, but turned up their noses at guys like Cole. Unless they knew the size of his bank account.

Chatting with Lindsay, he'd been surprised to find

the morning rush hour drive to Phoenix pass in a blip. He couldn't say he really knew anything more about her life, other than the tidbits on her website that gave glimpses into her artist soul, but he felt as though he knew *her*.

That she was genuine. Truly kind.

Could be kidding himself.

He didn't think so.

He handed her off for her tour of the plant because he'd had to. He hadn't wanted to. But he'd made appointments to see a couple of employees who'd had matters to discuss with him. His people came before personal wishes.

Most particularly when there was no solid basis for wishing.

Not only was the woman a new hire, an employee, she was way out of his league. Enjoying her company— that he could do. Seeing that she was comfortable, making her laugh—ditto. All areas in which he excelled.

But feeling compelled to be with her?

Big fat nada.

Been there. Done that.

Life was too short for any more false promises to himself.

Only a stupid man refused to learn from past events and set himself up for heartbreak over and over. Cole might not be the handsomest guy on the block, but he was a very wise one.

Which was why he chose not to suggest to Lindsay that they hang around for a nice lunch in the city before heading back to Shelter Valley after they'd conducted their separate business at the plant. He didn't need any temptation to encourage a friendship between him and his new hire.

Other than to keep her happy in the job, and do what he could to introduce her to Shelter Valley life so she'd hang around. At least long enough to work up her own line of Christmas cards. Per Brent, the night before.

After Cole had told his boss, mentor and friend about the cards he'd viewed during his last interview. Showed him the photo he'd taken of them.

And to both ends, keeping boundaries around himself, and discussing the business he had with her, he asked, "So what did you think?" as he turned his SUV toward the city freeway that would lead them to the state highway back to Shelter Valley just after eleven that Friday morning.

He listened with satisfaction, pleasure and then… more as she enthused about every aspect of her tour. The quality of materials, the state-of-the-art machinery and tools—and the obvious pride that the employees all took in their work. She'd homed in on the core of his job. A physically and emotionally healthy work environment. Happy employees.

Her comments were all about others. Not herself. As she spoke, the thing that kept coming back to him was that her excitement revolved around what she'd like to contribute to Elite Paper, not what the company could do for her. And he found himself enamored all over again.

"You want to stop and get some lunch before we leave the city?" he asked her, slowing to get off the freeway. "I know a family-owned Mexican place not far from here that serves the best…everything. It's a small place, in a strip mall. Nothing fancy…"

And was gratified some more when she turned that beautiful smile on him and said, "That sounds wonderful, thank you."

In the parking lot, walking beside her, feeling like a giant towering over her slim perfection, Cole kept his hands in his pockets and reminded himself once again that she was only a work associate. The lunch was a welcome-to-the-company thing, and a practical thing—since it would be after lunch by the time they got back to Shelter Valley—not a pleasure thing.

Absolutely not a personal thing.

As life would have it, the place was crowded—mostly with businesspeople from the skirts and ties around them—and the only thing available to them was a booth. Which meant spreading his legs wide enough that his knees weren't constantly bumping hers, and trying to maneuver so his stomach wasn't touching the edge of the ceramic-tiled table.

"You want to move?" Lindsay asked him before he'd even had a chance to open his menu. "I'm fine to wait for a table."

Her smile radiated empathy—but not repulsion or even judgment.

"I'm fine," he told her. And other than that initial moment of embarrassment when he'd slid into the booth, he really was. "It looks worse than it is," he said to her with a grin. Adding, "There's still plenty of room for me to squeeze in a full-size chimichanga plate. Which I highly recommend by the way."

His comfort in the booth—personal conversation, and therefore frowned upon. The menu—not personal, so safe.

They ordered drinks. Both looking at the menu. Didn't matter that he had it memorized and already knew what he wanted. He was keeping his focus off a potential new friend who would never be more than that.

Just until he was absolutely certain he wasn't going off the rails. He couldn't remember a time when he was so immediately aware of the emotions emanating from another person.

The drinks came.

While Lindsay ordered, rather than watching how she seemed to make the waitress feel comfortable, how she took time to compliment the older woman on her jewelry with what came off as complete sincerity, rather than allowing himself to risk a relapse into liking his lunch mate too much, Cole set himself an agenda for the lunch.

Purely business. Present their new employee with his boss's proposal from the night before. If they were going to get holiday cards produced with the quality required by Elite's owner, there was no time to waste.

Finished delivering his own order, Cole turned back to facing straight ahead after conversing with their waitress, and his gaze collided with the brown eyes across from him. While she watched him, Lindsay was stirring her straw in her soda. Around and around. Over and over.

It was almost like he could feel her tension. Or doubt?

The woman was not only gorgeous to look at, she was a truly gifted artist. And yet, had no confidence?

Was second-guessing herself?

Someone must have done a real number on her.

Which got his dander up.

"Several people mentioned Brent Wilson this morning." Her words, not his own mandates or self-control, brought him back out of the quagmire he kept trying to fall into with her.

Ironically, on the exact track he'd just set for the business lunch to follow. Almost as though she'd received a copy of the agenda.

"Is he really as focused on quality as everyone seems to think?" She'd stopped stirring as she looked over at him, giving him the impression that the future rested on his answer.

"Absolutely," he looked her straight in the eye with that one. "The man has had multiple offers to be publicly traded, which would likely make him a billionaire overnight, but he refuses to do so because he knows that the minute he does, a board will take over and profits will then drive every single decision made."

Straw moving again.

He noticed.

And leaned forward, ready to do whatever it took to make her feel as comfortable, as safe in her new life choices and changes, as she seemed to try to do for everyone around her.

Brent Wilson, Elite Paper Company, gave him perfect fodder. His own confidence in his ability to help women assured him that he could get the job done.

Sometimes life was about more than smart personal choices. Sometimes a guy just had to do what he could to help an obviously struggling person through a difficult transition.

Because he could.

## Chapter Three

"The man seems too good to be true," Lindsay said aloud what she'd been thinking all morning, as Cole took a break from his long list of business choices, loaded with anecdotes, relating to Brent Wilson. Both as a business owner, and as a man.

Lunch had arrived. While it was as good as Cole had promised, she'd picked at it. Spicy food wasn't cohabitating nicely with her knotted stomach. Growing knottier by the second.

She almost told him to stop talking. To change the subject. If she believed half of what he was telling her about various work situations where Brent had intervened, or ideas he'd had, policies he'd made and promises he'd kept, the man who'd fathered her was a saint.

She knew better than that.

Saints didn't run out on their responsibilities. Leav-

ing a frightened, emotionally sensitive young woman to
deal with a pregnancy—and her disappointed parents—
on her own.

After excusing herself to the restroom to escape the
praise parade, she splashed her face with cool water.
Bent at the knees so the hand dryer attached to the wall
could dry her skin.

What was she doing?

Or better yet, why?

How could she want to meet such a horrible human
being? Claim him as her own?

But if he was half the man he seemed to be, how
could she walk away? The not knowing would eat at
her for the rest of her life.

She had the thought as another woman pushed
through the bathroom door. And she let herself out,
knowing she'd just hit on her answer.

It wasn't about her having a relationship with the
man who'd fathered her. Or even knowing him. It was
about being done with the not knowing.

So she could put the broken parts of herself to rest.

And find a way to let the parts that were smothering
fly instead.

What that meant, or how it would look, practically,
in her real life, she had no idea. And that was part of the
problem. She expected herself to always know.

Her entire life was one regimented plan. Including
regularly scheduled appointments—weekends away—
to help Lindsay Warren breathe.

Reaching the booth feeling back on task, she sat down

with new purpose. To know. Whatever was there. No preconceived notions.

And only one sure boundary. No one was to get hurt. Not even her father. And certainly not his family. What he'd done before them had been no choice of theirs.

She could know without telling.

Leave town with her knowledge, but give none up to others.

"You okay?" Cole asked, still working on his large plate of food.

"Fine," she told him, smiling, as she presented herself to her own lunch with a new appetite. Set to enjoy the moment as she worked on gathering her knowledge.

It didn't all have to happen at once. She had a month.

She would get the lay of the land and then figure out a way to naturally bump into Brent Wilson—employee to employer only.

Maybe that was all it would take.

"Brent wants you to design an entire line for Christmas."

Fork suspended, she stared at the large redheaded man glancing at her. She was completely unprepared.

More knowledge regarding Brent Wilson's life than she needed. What he wanted...not part of her search.

"Don't look so shocked," Cole said, smiling that captivating smile again. How a look could make her want to crawl inside it and stay there, she had no idea. But it did. "You're an incredible artist, Lindsay. The way you see ordinary things, express what's there, what we all know is there, but with dimensions us regular guys don't see..."

"There is nothing regular about you, Cole Bennet," she said, mostly because she had to lighten a moment that was threatening to bring tears to her eyes. Her father wanted her to design her own Christmas line? She swallowed hard, and said, "I heard as much about you as I did about Mr. Wilson." Her words came out sounding to her as though they'd been announced on a loudspeaker in a filled-to-capacity sports arena. But she kept rambling. "I heard you single-handedly broke up a domestic dispute last year out in the parking lot. You managed to de-escalate some guy who was over the edge due to an emotional break."

He put down his fork. Wiped his mouth. Nodded.

"Okay, yeah, I did that, but they make it sound like more than it was. It's not like he had a gun or anything."

"No, from what I heard he had his hands around her throat." She'd heard it from the woman he'd saved. Elite's production manager of more than ten years. Not knowing that her husband had just lost his entire life savings in a high stakes card game, she'd told him by phone an hour earlier that she was filing for divorce.

"He wasn't a violent guy," Cole said then, as though that somehow made his intervention less valuable. "I've known him for years. Had never, in any way, shown physical aggression with her. He had a gambling problem he couldn't get on top of."

"You saved him from himself." Lindsay said the words softly, as she was thinking them. The man's strange effect on her had done that to her a few times in the short while she'd known him. Had her just blurting out her thoughts without filters. It was like all of the normal guards she held up evaporated around him.

Or she was just feeling particularly vulnerable.

Which made more sense.

"So…was all that distraction your way of saying you aren't interested in taking on a project as big as your own line? In time for production for a holiday lay down?"

"It's July. How could that happen in such a short period of time?"

"We'd have to limit the number of cards to fit one production line, keep them all within the same medium and probably only offer them to key accounts that first year…"

Wow. Her mind raced. Or rather, Lindsay Warren's did. Her fake persona was giving him a big silent *hell, yes.* And was wanting to jump up and kiss the man.

Her own line of cards? Produced by a company with one of the highest reputations in the business? It was a dream come true. One she'd never even let herself dream through to the end.

The real Lindsay reined in Ms. Bohemian, as she sometimes thought of the alter ego who'd been pushing at Lindsay's edges her entire life. "What kind of deadline are we talking?" she asked. Just to be polite.

And because she was weak. Wanting another few minutes to let the artist lurking inside her bask in sweet possibility.

Cole's grin melted her again. Probably a bohemian residual. Maybe that was what all of her uncharacteristic responses and reactions to him were about. The thought struck like lightning. And stuck, too. That explained it. Lindsay Warren had been set free for more than a weekend at a small art show in a random park. She'd been given the reins to live completely.

Ms. Bohemian, not Lindsay Warren-Smythe, was overreacting emotionally to the great man they'd just met...

"A month?" The man asked, eyebrows raised, smile still fully in place, as he made the ridiculous request.

"Okay." The word was out before Lindsay could calculate, formulate, mark off time.

"Okay?" He sat straighter. Even chuckled. "Seriously?"

No. She didn't think so. But wipe that look off his face? "Yes," she said. "I can do it." Neither of the Lindsays had any doubt about that.

The real one just wasn't sure she should even try.

Because as much as she'd love to let her inner heart fly on its own, she didn't see how it would work, her father carrying a line of her pseudonym's work without him eventually figuring out who she really was.

And there was no place yet, in her current plan, for that to happen.

So much for Cole's plan to remain distant from Lindsay Warren. All the way back to Shelter Valley she was like a fluorescent light sparkling colors that touched everything around her. No way could a guy ignore something like that.

She spouted ideas, wondering how to bring various nebulous things, like the love and excitement of a present under the tree, to the naked eye, and then coming up with ways to make it happen. Talking about raised paper, three-dimensional embellishments. Colors. Asking specific questions about some production limitations, smiling when she heard there were none on some of the ideas she was coming up with.

Everything about her intrigued him. But as he pulled into Shelter Valley, disappointed that he had to drop her off to her own transportation, he felt as though he was setting a child free and giving a huge responsibility to someone he fully trusted to get it done. She talked a mile a minute about her own vision. And then asked practical questions about processes, even some tools and supplies, that he'd have expected her to know far more about than he did.

"Brent's having a barbecue tomorrow afternoon at his place," he said, feeling the pressure of knowing he only had half a mile left before she'd be out of his car. "All of the management of Elite has been invited, but there will be even more people from Shelter Valley there..." Thinking aloud, he just kept talking. "You have any interest in coming as my guest?" *No! Sounded too much like a date.* "In light of your now incredibly tight deadline, and a schedule that's been severely escalated, it would give you a chance to meet key company people face-to-face, in a relaxed setting. And give you a crash course in Shelter Valley life, too. You know, so there will be familiar faces as you settle into town."

*Good save, man.*

She obviously thought so, judging by her nod. "That makes a lot of sense. I'd love to go. What time? Where? And what's the dress code?"

He couldn't help the grin that spread across his big round face. "Two. I'll pick you up. And this is Arizona in the summertime. We're casual. A lot of people will be swimming, so you can bring a suit if you'd like. Otherwise, cool and comfortable. Brent has outdoor misters and portable air conditioners, but in the direct sun, it'll still be hot."

He was breaking out in a sweat just thinking about what he'd let himself in for as he pulled up beside her old, but surprisingly fresh and snappy, yellow car in the parking lot behind Elite Paper's home office.

If someone got the wrong idea, thought he was moving in on the town's newest beautiful woman before anyone else got a chance...because, of course, that would likely be the only way he could get her...

"I'll be ready at two," she told him, opening her door. "With so much to do in such a short time, I'm going to go in right now and get settled into my office. And thank you so much for today. For lunch. Everything."

She was out of the car, a beauty who moved with a model's grace, heading toward the building before he realized he hadn't responded.

With so much new coming at her, and the strong possibility of the project of her life actually being on the table, Lindsay sailed through the rest of the Friday. Stayed busy in her new little office off the art room at Elite Paper Company Headquarters until she was told the building was closing down for the night.

At which time she texted Cole to ask him if it was possible for her to get access to the place after hours.

Her phone rang less than a minute later. His number on the screen.

"Are you still on the property?"

"In my workspace," she told him, unable to call the small room an actual office. "I was just told I have to leave."

"Stay put," he said. "I'll be there in a few."

Happy to keep exploring canvas with many of the supplies she'd found, but never used, Lindsay was lost within the visions inside her head when she heard Cole's voice again.

"Hey."

Her jump sent her brush across the eleven-by-fourteen canvas, and slid the palette smeared with a mixture of glitter, glue and paint to the floor.

"I am so sorry," he told her, crouching to pick up the palette. "I didn't mean to scare you."

Seeing the back of his curly head, the huge shoulders, bending over the results of her playtime, she quickly dropped her canvas in the large trash can on the other side of her stool. "It's not your fault," she assured him. "You spoke softly."

His glance up at her, a quirky grin, had her smiling right back at him.

"I've only ever worked alone." She found herself giving him a glimpse into her real life. "In a private studio." One big room in a professional building a couple hours' north of her La Jolla home, rented by Lindsay Warren. Lindsay had a little weekend getaway, a one-room apartment, a block from the building.

Sitting there, looking up as Cole stood, Lindsay felt

for a second like she was falling apart, right there in that little room.

Her life…so clean and compartmentalized, so predictable…seemed a mass of separated pieces as she saw how she might look through the eyes of the chief of personnel of a highly reputable company.

"I won't keep you," he said then, laying a key card down on her desk. "This will get you into the building when it's locked, and give you access to the second floor, too, if you swipe it in the elevator. It's programmed to you, so, obviously, don't loan it out, and report it missing immediately if you lose it."

Feeling like she should stand—Lindsay Warren-Smythe would most definitely be standing—Lindsay sat there looking at him. Nodding.

Wanting him to find her worthy of the trust he was placing in her. Doubting that he would if he knew why she was there.

Ironic, considering that Lindsay Warren-Smythe was the owner of a couple of buildings whose occupants gave out key cards to their employees. And she had twenty-four-hour fingerprint access to many others.

She was still stuck on the incident several hours later as she sat alone in her little Shelter Valley apartment. She'd left Elite shortly after Cole exited her space with a reminder that he'd pick her up at two the next day.

Following signs in town, she'd driven out to the hiking trail winding around a smallish mountain peak on the edge of Shelter Valley. Had thought about walking it a short distance, but the oppressive heat and her flip-flops had convinced her otherwise.

She'd walked around downtown, instead, ending up at Montford University in the center of town. Had spent time wandering the impressive campus, passed more time in the library and eventually ended up back at her apartment.

Not having had a single conversation.

What did Lindsay Warren, an imaginary woman, have to say?

With questions bombarding her, she thought of Savannah, only an hour away, in Phoenix. The woman was married to her job, lived alone, just like Lindsay did, which was part of what had bonded the two in the beginning.

Not that Savannah was ever really alone. Her partners at Sierra's Web were as much family to her as any biologically related people Lindsay had ever known.

Still, having had her cell phone in hand for several minutes, she dialed.

"Everything okay?" Savannah picked up before the second ring. Of course. She was on Lindsay's payroll at the moment, and there was the whole married-to-the-job thing.

"This is a personal call," she stipulated right up front.

"Doesn't change my question. Everything okay?"

"I don't know."

"Where are you?"

"The apartment." And then, because she had apartments in other places, and was letting her mind implode on her, she added, "In Shelter Valley."

"You think you've been made?"

"No. Just the opposite." Hearing the distress in her

voice, something that Warren-Smythe never let show, she asked, "Am I doing anything wrong here?"

"Legally, you mean?"

No. But, "Okay." She trusted Savannah to have all of that covered. But maybe hearing it would snap her out of the morass into which she'd fallen.

"You are absolutely not breaking any laws," Savannah told her. "Lindsay Warren has been established as an artist for as long as she says she has. We got you legally set up with your LLC, and had it registered with the business bureau before you ever went to your first show. Your studio, your apartment, all rented under and paid for by the LLC. And at Elite, technically you were hired as an on-site contractor, not an employee, with monies going into Lindsay Warren, LLC."

Which was why she hadn't had to provide a social security number. Her website, established four years before, her LLC registry naming Lindsay Warren as a manager, along with people with whom Lindsay Warren had done business for references, had been her credentials. A bank account number registered to the LLC was provided for payment. All neatly clean and aboveboard.

Thanks to Savannah.

"But you already knew all of that."

"Yeah."

"Do I need to come there and get you?"

That snapped her back to sanity. "Of course not."

"So, talk."

"Wait, are you at dinner or anything? Am I interrupting?"

"I'm home eating take-out Chinese and planning a

candlelit hot soak in the tub with a glass of wine, some of the homemade bubbles gifted to me by Lindsay Warren, LLC and Voice of the Feminine Spirit playing in the background."

All of which Lindsay should have been doing.

Would do as soon as she hung up. Minus the Chinese takeout. She'd brought home a veggie sub, purchased from the grocery deli case and paid for at self-checkout.

"I feel like a creep, deceiving sincere people."

"Are you Lindsay Warren, the artist?"

"Of course."

"Do you suffer pangs of guilt when you're at art shows?"

"Never."

Silence hung on the line.

Lindsay got the unspoken message hanging there.

"I'm only at shows for a weekend, tops," she finally said. "The people I meet are in and out of my life."

"What about Trevor Burnside?"

The seventy-year-old glassblower was a wise man. Living in Canada. They'd met at a show she'd done in northern Washington State. They emailed. Often.

"That's different."

"How?"

"He doesn't expect any more than email. For evermore. I can deliver on that promise."

"So what you're saying is that someone there is expecting more than you can deliver?"

No. But…

And there she was at the crux of her problem. She

couldn't wrap her mind around what would come after that *but*.

"Have you promised something you can't provide?"

"No, of course not." She'd get the Christmas line done. With joy. Couldn't wait to really get started on it. Had been flowing with ideas up until Cole Bennet had shown up with the damned key card.

Which spoke permanence.

"We purposely brought you in as a contractor, Lins, for just this purpose. If the job hadn't posted that way, we'd have done something else. You're transitory."

The people at Elite weren't treating her like she was. Cole wasn't.

"I was invited to a company—actually, town, too—barbecue tomorrow afternoon. At Wilson's house."

"Ohhhh."

"What?"

"I'd call Kelly to have a chat with you, but we don't need an expert psychiatrist to figure this one out," Savannah said softly, her tone filled with the compassion that she reserved for those she cared personally about. "You're meeting your father tomorrow, Lins. You'd be more of a worry to me if you weren't struggling tonight."

Made sense. Glorious, logical sense.

"That's what this is about?" she asked then.

"What else could it be? You're in a town where you know basically no one. Working with people you've only just met..."

A flash of Cole Bennet's face passed before her mind's eye, but she let it go. Was glad to know that she could.

Had valid reason to do so.

Cole just stood for the specter of meeting the man who'd fathered her. He was the means by which she and Sierra's Web were making that happen.

Her incongruent and oddly vulnerable feelings where he was concerned were about meeting her father.

Lindsay was already pouring her wine and reaching for her sandwich, on the way to run her bath as Savannah told her to get some rest, and to call her as soon as she was home from the barbecue the next day. Sooner if needed.

It wasn't until she was naked in the tub, sipping wine, when thoughts of Cole Bennet took over all mental space, that she really got it.

He was a distraction. And a secure, safe, legal and legitimate means to finish the task she'd started.

If she needed to entertain completely private, totally sexual fantasies of the big red-headed man to distract her from trauma coming her way, then she'd go ahead and let them occupy all her brain waves. As long as no one else knew, who was she hurting?

## Chapter Four

Feeling the movement of warm weight away from his back, Cole awoke Saturday morning with a sense of anticipation he didn't immediately place. The nudge at his neck brought him to full consciousness in the king-sized bed he shared every night.

"Okay, Lillie, I'm up," he said groggily. Cole loved living life. But he loved sleeping, too. Started to drift off again. Another nudge had him throwing back the covers and sitting up.

Looking to the side of him, grinning, he said, "Okay, now I'm up. You satisfied?"

The ten-year-old rough collie nudged his elbow, and he grinned. Rubbing behind her ears just as she'd taught him to do. And then she lay on the bed and kept watch as he showered, shaved and climbed into a pair of loose tan cotton shorts and pulled on one of his favorite purple tank tops. The thinnest, softest one he owned. As he slid into his flip-flops, Lillie jumped off the bed and ran to her doggy door, let herself outside into his large desert-landscaped backyard to do her business in the grassy area that had been laid just for her.

He made his coffee. Scrambled the eggs he and Lillie shared every morning, and had hers in her bowl, mixed in with the senior dry food, by the time she came back inside. The girl had her morning routine. Alarm clock. Shower-watch duty. Her business. Check every inch of the walled-in half-acre backyard, including the entire rim of the built-in pool, and then in for breakfast.

Cole, sitting at the granite breakfast bar in his kitchen—because the high stools let him sit comfortably with his feet touching the floor, rather than cramming his knees under the table— took his time with his own eggs, toast, oatmeal and orange juice. Conversing with Lillie, as always.

Telling her the day's agenda.

Convinced that she understood enough of what he was saying to make his choice to share it with her valid. The way she sat there, cocking her head, her ears, as he spoke, paying intense intention, was proof enough for him.

"We've got a party thing at Brent and Emily's today, girl," he told her. And would swear to the fact that she nodded once. Acknowledging her part in the day's activities.

She'd be the only canine family member at the event, but a lot of people would be disappointed if she wasn't there. Since the first year he'd adopted Lillie from a puppy mill rescue, she'd been an expected companion, accompanying him even to work on many occasions.

Motioning with his fork as he swallowed a bite of toast and egg, he continued with the most important part. "You're going to meet someone new," he said, his eating paused as he gave Lillie his full focus. "She's a new hire, just moved to town, and we want her to like it here."

Cocking her head to the side, Lillie seemed to be waiting for more.

"It's not a personal thing, though," he quickly assured her. "Not like she'll be trespassing on our turf here. She's doesn't have any friends yet, so we're going to introduce her around." He took a bite then. A big one. Followed by a spoonful of oatmeal.

Lillie watched.

"She's nice," he said. Took another bite. Wanted more jelly on his toast and got up to get the jar. Took care of the problem.

All under the watchful eye of one of the smartest females he'd ever known.

And it hit him. "You might actually be able to help, you know," he told her. "Lindsay's a gifted artist. I'm talking talent like I've never seen except in museums. You don't just see her work, you feel it."

The dog sat back and scratched her ear.

Okay, he'd segued out of canine territory.

"She's beautiful, too," he said, anyway. Just to get that part out of the way so he could move forward to Lillie's part.

"She's afraid of something," he said then, baldly, giving Lillie a serious look. The girl stopped scratching immediately. Sat up straight, watching him.

Almost like she was asking him to expound on what he'd told her.

"I don't know what," he said. "But you'll know what I mean when you see her."

Because, true to her breed, Lillie had become an excellent service dog. Even before Cole had taken her for formal training at the program offered by the vet clinic in town. The girl sensed when someone's heart rate increased, when they were agitated.

And she knew how to intervene.

Yes. It was perfect. Him picking up Lindsay Warren later that afternoon, taking her to a party to which she hadn't actually been invited, it all made good sense.

He was doing his part to help his new hire acclimate in an attempt to keep her happy. Happy employees were his end goal. Said so in his job description. And if that meant providing one with an afternoon under the care of a service dog who'd make her transition to Shelter Valley a more comfortable one, then so be it.


What did a twenty-eight-year-old woman wear to meet her father for the first time?

The two-thousand-dollar diamond hoop earrings her grandfather bought for her when she graduated from college? Or the antique sapphire and diamond white gold necklace Mimi gave her last Christmas?

Lindsay couldn't wear either. The earrings were locked in her safe at home in La Jolla. And the necklace, because it had belonged to her mimi's mimi, Lindsay's great-great-grandmother, was in Lindsay's vault at the bank.

Both pieces were Warren-Smythe all the way.

The person she desperately needed to be as she stepped onto the property of the man who'd deserted her emotionally fragile mother.

Because, apparently, in spite of what he'd done, she was still driven to know the part of herself that had been missing all her life.

Lindsay Warren had no standoffish clothes. Nothing that established clear boundaries.

Something that calmed her swarming stomach would be good.

But as Lindsay looked over the two suitcases' worth of colorful expressive clothes—the entirety of Lindsay Warren's wardrobe—she couldn't find anything that calmed her, either.

After trying on three different outfits, she settled for the fourth. A thin cotton red-and-white tie-dyed spaghetti-strap dress that hung to her ankles. She liked the soft feel of it swirling against her skin as she moved. And the red jeweled flip-flops she wore with it were her favorites.

Three pairs of thin red metal flowers, dangling to various lengths, adorned her ears. Her hair she left loose, a shroud to hide within, protecting her.

She'd spent the early morning hours back out at the trail she'd visited the night before, walking up the winding pavement to a railed lookout with benches. And then, still in bike shorts and crop top, had stopped at

Elite headquarters to make a few sketches that had come to her during the outing.

Fulfilling her purpose. And her promise.

She'd eaten fruit and vegetables. Had some chamomile tea.

And still, as she stood out in the parking lot of the apartment complex, watching for Cole's SUV to pull in, she was a weak mass of nerves.

Being attacked by guilt.

Cole wasn't just a ride to a party. Or a boss. He was different, though she couldn't explain why or how to herself, which was why she hadn't been able to discuss him with Savannah the night before.

She felt like she was using him—because that's how she knew it would appear from the outside looking in.

And yet, she was doing nothing wrong. She'd accepted an invitation from her new boss. The fact that she took personal pleasure from time spent with him wasn't something she could help.

She just had to make sure that she didn't send off vibes that gave him more than friendship pleasure.

Even if she was curious about that "more." A lot curious.

He was a specter. And a distraction. He was also a very sexy living and breathing human being.

All of her emotional edginess aside, she'd never been so instantly attracted to a man in her entire life. Trauma over meeting her father could account for her vulnerability where Cole was concerned. Her unusual sense of relating to him. No way could the trauma be responsible for increased libido.

So, okay. She'd acknowledged the situation. Admitted it to herself. All she had to do was manage it so that Cole Bennet didn't suffer from knowing her.

Her thoughts stopped abruptly when she caught a brief glimpse of his SUV pulling into the parking lot before it was blocked by the buildings directly across from hers. There'd been movement in the passenger seat of the car.

*And there you have it.* She wasn't the only person Cole was taking to the party. Wouldn't even be riding in the front seat.

So much for needing to worry about leading him on.

He had himself covered.

"Back." Cole said the one word as he spotted Lindsay standing outside her building.

As soon as he pulled to a stop, Lillie jumped into the rear seat.

If the girl caught his sudden intake of breath, the way his entire being swept with a wave of anticipation, she didn't say so. Lillie was too busy watching the gorgeous woman in her flowing dress approaching the vehicle.

The dog wouldn't have noticed how the thin fabric of Lindsay's dress clung to her perfectly shaped legs as she walked, but Cole had.

With some physical discomfort.

Pulling at the bottom of his shirt, making certain that it was covering vital parts, he grinned as Lindsay opened the back door to greet Lillie.

"Oh!" Her surprise as the girl nodded, and then watched her calmly, sent Cole's grin to a full-blown smile. Lindsay sounded happy to see the beautiful canine. Lillie had that effect on people.

"Lindsay, meet Lillie." Seemed like the formal introduction was appropriate.

He watched as his new contracted employee buried her face in Lillie's neck, kissing the side of her face, before saying, "I'm glad to make your acquaintance, Lillie."

A natural dog person.

He wasn't at all surprised.

"I've never heard of a party where people bring their pets," she said, as she buckled herself into the front seat. Her words, issued with a smile, held approval.

"This isn't one," he warned. "Lillie's going to be the only canine there."

"Oh." She didn't say anything more.

He wanted her to. It would be nice if she'd offered an anecdote or two about herself.

There were things he wanted to know. Like, "Did you have a dog growing up?"

Clearly, she didn't currently have one. The apartment complex where she was staying didn't allow pets.

"No." That was it. No expansion on the subject.

"What about later? When you were out on your own?"

"No. Growing up, though, I wanted a collie. Lassie and all."

The show was before their time.

And so much for her being a dog person.

"Lillie's kind of a community dog," he told her then, just to pass the time while they made the short drive out of the middle of town to the road of estate homes by the east mountain. "Our local vet, Cassie Montford—you'll meet her today, she's the wife of the son of the town's founder—she runs a rescue clinic. When Lillie came in, I couldn't pass her up. The girl was in rough shape, couldn't be left alone for the first several months of her life and went with me everywhere. Everyone kind of adopted her. Since then she's had therapy training. We do stints at the nursing home, and accept invitations from shut-ins, or, like when one of the local kids broke her leg in gymnastics, we did biweekly visits at her home, that kind of thing."

Lindsay's smile, as she watched him and glanced back at Lillie a few times too, kept him talking. "And, you'll soon notice, she thinks she lives at Brent and Emily's too, as do their kids. Anytime I have to be gone overnight, she stays with them."

The smile was gone. Lindsay's gaze faced the windshield.

Something he'd said?

And it struck him. Brent and Emily were family to him. To much of the town. But to Lindsay, Brent Wilson was the owner of the company who'd just contracted her to work for them. And based on Cole's impressions over the past day and a half, the job at Elite meant a great deal to Lindsay. Maybe even more than her working for them meant to Elite.

Which was saying a lot.

He'd yet to figure out why, when based on her skill she should have had her pick of jobs, she'd been so eager to grab at theirs. What had happened to make her so hesitant, so…nervous and eager to please?

None of his business.

And yet, being him, he'd likely find out. And do what he could to help ease her way.

It was who he was. What he did.

And he liked that about himself.

The long drive, the massive desert-landscaped front yard—complete with water fountain and flowing river— the castle-like beige stucco home including turrets might have impressed Lindsay Warren, if she hadn't been living inside Warren-Smythe her entire life.

Her father had done well for himself.

But then she'd already known that.

About to come up out of her skin as she noticed the paved driveway filled with cars, saw others coming up behind them, Lindsay felt a nudge at her neck.

Jerked. And then…settled.

Reaching her hand up, she laid it against the warmth of Lillie's neck. Offered the rescue girl the love and affection Lindsay would have liked to have had from a father.

Felt a wet nose at the back of her ear as Cole parked.

And remembered what he'd said about Lillie's service training. Glancing at Cole then, afraid the dog was giving her away, that Cole would think she was vulnerable, she was glad to see him fully occupied with backing his SUV into the very tight spot.

"Is she this friendly with everyone?" she asked then, just to clearly establish that she and the dog were just getting to know one another, not that Lillie was being of service.

"Yep," Cole told her with a grin as he put the vehicle in Park and pushed the button to shut off the ignition. Ruffling the dog's ear, he continued, "Don't be surprised if she checks back with you a time or two, though. You were in her car and you're new to her. She might need to explore that situation."

His accompanying chuckle warmed her. Almost as much as the thought of Lillie hanging out with her some over the next difficult minutes without alerting anyone that Lindsay might be a bit emotionally vulnerable.

She didn't need the dog to get through the upcoming ordeal.

Warren-Smythe would be there, able to handle whatever transpired.

And she didn't need Cole Bennet in her life, either. He was a great guy she was lucky to associate with while she completed an assignment.

What she needed, she discovered as she opened the car door and attempted to stand, was a bit of strength in her suddenly weak knees. Grabbing the back door handle, as Cole greeted an older man getting out of the car next to them, she freed Lillie from the SUV. And when Lillie nudged her hand, she lightly stroked the dog's head.

Hated that such a sweet thing had been abused to the point of needing round-the-clock care for months. She'd never done fundraising for therapy or rescue animals, but as soon as she got home, she was going to look into doing so, pro bono. If nothing else, she'd volunteer and donate.

Having given up on a dog of her own as a kid, she'd moved on. Focused on what she could have instead of longing for what she couldn't.

And there she was, meeting the father she'd given up on. And having a dog make her acquaintance, too.

Maybe she should have just stayed home and gotten a dog.

"Lindsay, there's someone I'd like you to meet," Cole called out to her, standing with another set of new arrivals. A couple in their sixties, she'd guess. Both dressed casually, wearing welcoming smiles, and…holding hands with each other.

"This is Becca and Will Parsons," Cole said, holding out an arm to draw Lindsay up to them. "Becca's the mayor of Shelter Valley and Will is president of Montford University."

Whoa. Daddy Wilson didn't mess around.

She nodded, smiled a gracious Warren-Smythe smile, held out her hand and expressed how pleased she was to meet them. Completely confident for the minute or two the four of them stood in conversation.

Too soon, the Parsonses moved on to other arrivals, and Cole motioned for him and Lindsay to join the random small groups of people meandering toward a sidewalk that led to a gate at the side of a five-car garage.

"Where's Lillie?" She hadn't meant the question to come out with such alarm. But had thought she'd have the dog beside her when she entered the backyard.

"Probably inside, saying hello to Kaitlin, Kerby and Kyle."

Her father's children. Savannah had given her the rundown. Names and ages. Kaitlin thirteen, Kyle fifteen, Kerby eleven.

Her half brothers and sister.

She missed a step.

Grabbing her by the arm with his left hand, Cole slid his right behind her back. Steadying her.

The shock of his touch whistled through her as she said, "Sorry, my flip-flop slid off the walk…"

The words weren't right. Warren-Smythe would have thanked him for his gallantry and moved away.

Ms. Bohemian let him continue to keep his hand lightly at her back as he led her through the gate.

## Chapter Five

The lovely two-acre backyard was already alive with people milling about. Groups sat at tables around the pool, Will Parsons's sister Randi was in the pool with Becca and Will's twins—miracle babies who were both recent Montford graduates.

"Brent and Emily are still inside," Cole told Lindsay. "They have some of the food catered, but do all of the serving themselves. I generally help with that—you want to join me?"

"Who's that?" Lindsay asked, smiling at Martha and Reverend Marks as they came in the gate and passed them by.

"David and Martha Marks. He's the preacher at the big white church in the center of town. She was a single mother whose daughter had been attacked when the reverend first came to town. He fell in love with the family, and they with him. And just for full exposure, I'm not telling you anything the entire town doesn't already know. Martha's daughter is happily married now. She's the kindergarten teacher here in town."

When Elite's HR manager came through the gate with her husband, and Lindsay smiled at them, saying hello, Cole asked her once again if she wanted to come inside with him. Thinking it would be easier for her to meet the company's owner in a smaller, private setting.

"No," she told him, glancing over as Lillie came out onto the patio by the pool. "You go ahead. I'll be fine out here."

When he hesitated, she smiled at him. "Seriously, Mr. Bennet. I appreciate your effort to make sure I'm comfortable, but you don't have to babysit me. Go. Enjoy yourself. I'm going to do what you brought me here to do. Meet some of the people for whom I'll be working, and some of the people around whom I'll be living."

Her expression, the tone in her voice...they were different. Almost as though he was being dismissed.

Cole went into the house to seek out Brent and Emily, to offer his services, as always. But he did so with a backward glance. Watching as Lindsay made her way forward into the throng. What had that been about?

Had he come on too strong?

Read more into their new employer/employee comradery than had been there?

Offended her somehow?

And then he saw where she was headed, who she stopped to talk to, and he understood.

Lillie to the rescue.

With a nod toward his girl, and a smile back on his face, Cole went to grab the heavily laden tray his friends had waiting for him.

Lindsay knew what the man looked like. Savannah's portfolio had included a family photo from an article done on Elite Paper. And a second from a social media post.

And there'd been the publicity shot of the man alone that she'd received from Sierra's Web after the DNA match had come through from a popular ancestry database.

She'd thought she was ready to see him in person. And, perhaps, if she'd been in an audience, waiting to hear him speak, she'd have done fine. As it was, the longer Cole was gone, meaning the sooner he'd reappear, most likely with Brent Wilson at his side, or soon following, the more agitated Lindsay became.

With Lillie staying close, she'd been able to maintain her Warren-Smythe upbringing enough to make conversation with half a dozen people. Had been introduced to the sheriff of Shelter Valley, Greg Richards, and his wife, Beth. Thought, if she'd been going to stay in town, she'd like to know Beth better. The woman seemed to know things she didn't show.

How Lindsay could ascertain that, she couldn't explain, even to herself. Told herself Ms. Bohemian was going overboard. Seeing things that most people didn't when viewing a sunset, for instance, was one thing. Seeing them in people was a bit much.

And with that thought—propelled by the opening

of the electric wall of sliding glass that led into a fully cooled patio where more than a dozen round tables were set—Lindsay ducked into the restroom cabana out by the pool.

Locking the door behind her, she stared at herself in the mirror. Looking for the person she'd been finding in the mirror her entire life. Saw her likeness.

And uncertainty in eyes that were generally filled with purpose.

"You don't have to do this," she told herself. Thought about how, logistically, she'd get out of the thronging backyard, and off the property, back to her apartment, without seeing the man that her ride was probably standing beside at that very moment.

"No one else knows." Her gaze cleared. Biology didn't show. Cole Bennet hadn't seemed shocked by her appearance, or made any reference to a likeness between Lindsay and his boss.

She was meeting her father, but to everyone else, including the man in question, she was just a new Elite employee at a summer weekend barbecue. All she had to do was smile and keep up appearances.

Something she'd been doing since she was old enough to follow simple direction.

Taking a couple of more minutes to cool down in the air-conditioned little room, to admire the mosaic tile on the walls, the matching Saltillo tile on the floor, Lindsay had her mind firmly on maintaining the poise she'd grown up perfecting as she opened the door.

Looking for Lillie, just because the girl sat down outside the bathroom door when Lindsay opened it to head in, she saw the dog a few yards away by the pool, leaning up against the leg of a tall, athletic-looking man with graying hair. She saw them from behind. The male hand on the dog's head.

"Lindsay!" Cole's voice brought her gaze upward, to the rest of the group standing with dog and man. "Come on over." The chief of personnel smiled as he issued the invitation. And she knew who Lillie had been affectionate with.

The moment was at hand.

All her life, she'd wondered—vacillating between anger and need whenever she thought about the unknown male who'd abandoned her and her mother—what the moment would look like if she ever met her father face-to-face.

Trepidation and an odd anticipation filled her, weighing her down. Her focus on Cole's smile wasn't a conscious thing. It just happened. She nodded.

Seemingly glued in the second. Not moving forward to the next one.

A bump at her hand drew her gaze from Cole's. Lillie's cold nose lifted Lindsay's palm, as though bringing her back to life. Petting the dog's head, she smiled and approached Cole, who was facing her. And saw the man with whom Cole had been standing turn around.

She knew the face, of course. A little more tanned than in the picture in the manila envelope at her apartment.

Lips trembling, heart pounding so hard she could feel the rapid beat, she approached. And her mimi's voice came to mind. Telling her how her father had left the state before she was even born.

Letting the anger take away any remnants of the lonely little girl in her heart, Lindsay met the man's gaze eye for eye. Tooth for tooth in her mind.

She heard Cole say, "Brent, this is Lindsay Warren. Lindsay, Brent Wilson…"

Eye to eye. Lillie's head beneath her hand. Brown eyes smiling into her own…brown eyes. Same round shape. Dark with that slight ring of lightening around the outer edges of the iris. Not something anyone would notice if they hadn't spent close to two decades staring at identical orbs every single morning as they drew lining on the lids atop and below them…

"I'm so delighted to meet you," the man said, his smile warm. Seemingly genuine. He didn't hold out a hand, for which she was grateful. "The photos Cole showed me of your work…you're good!"

Uh-huh. Good enough to work for you, but not…

No. Her fingers worked the fur around Lillie's ear. "Thank you for the opportunity to design my own line of cards." She said what she'd expect to hear if she was witnessing the interchange.

As far as she could wrap her mind around any such thought.

The man was…she couldn't even…

"Anything you need, you just let us know."

Stop smiling, she silently implored him.

You don't know who I am.

"I can't imagine what it would be," she said. Aware of the conversation, but hearing it as if through a globe of cotton.

No one knows. Keep up appearances. She smiled. It made her cheeks ache.

A million questions.

Pieces of a shattered heart.

Lillie's softness.

"Let's go get something to drink." Cole's voice. Pulling her out of the fog. She glanced at the man who stood a good three or four inches taller than the older man present. Was glad to be able to focus on one face without seeing the other.

"That would be great," she said, her smile hurting less as she focused on Cole's easy grin. "It was nice to meet you." She spoke the words by rote as they walked away.

Choking on the lie.

And finding truth there, too.

It was nice to have the meeting over.

And even better to take the glass of wine Cole Bennet was handing her.

"Cheers," he said, clicking his glass with hers, his ready grin steadying her, sliding inside her chest to ease the passageways.

*Thank you.* Her response was a silent smile back at him.


"I'm okay if you want to mingle with others." Lindsay's words were softly given.

At the buffet table, plates in hand after everyone else had served themselves, Cole glanced at the beautiful and yet oddly haunted looking face peering up at him. She'd been in a conversation with Sam and Cassie Montford when the buffet had officially opened, and

Cole had waited for her so she didn't have to go through the line alone.

"If I'm cramping you, just say so," he told her, taking a step back.

The instant flash of horror on her face was gone so fast he was glad he'd been watching acutely enough to see it. Was a bit put off by the placid, easygoing expression that covered it up. "Oh no, Cole! I just feel guilty, taking up so much of your time."

After studying her a few seconds longer, he shrugged, deciding to take her at face value. "These people have known me most of my life. See me every day. And know how to find me. Not a one of them will be upset that you're hogging my company." His chuckle came naturally, easing his own tension.

"More likely, they're watching to see if there's any spark between us," he added, with a conspiratorial wink. Watchers were hoping was more like it, though he'd long since taken the town's sympathetic view of his love life on the chin. "That would be the reason you might want some distance between us."

With a frown, she stared up at him. "Seriously?"

She'd chosen her food lightly. A spoonful of broccoli salad. A roll. Some kale stuff.

While he'd loaded his plate with barbecued pork, cooked potatoes. And two spoonfuls of broccoli salad. With one glass in one hand and an overladen plate in the other, he grabbed the first empty seat he came to. A cement bench by the pool. Not one of the mostly full tables. Others were eating at random spots other than the tables set up for the occasion. It always worked that way.

For Cole, it was practicality. The tables brought in were not only too short to fit his legs comfortably underneath, but they were also, by virtue of being portable, light enough that if his knee bumped into them from underneath, plates of food could end up in people's laps.

A fact learned the hard way.

And a circumstance that made it easier for him to choose to part ways with the woman whose company he was enjoying a little too much.

Her *"seriously"* still burned his ears. She was astounded that anyone would think she'd go for a guy like him?

Worried that some other more suitable potential new dates would think her taken?

There was no give in the cement bench to warn him that she'd joined him. Lillie's nose between their knees might have been a clue, if Cole hadn't already caught a whiff of the lavender-and-lilac whatever she used.

"I'm sorry, but I can't just let that last comment go," she said, her plate untouched while he shoved a forkful of meat and potatoes in his mouth. "Have I offended you somehow?"

For once, Cole wasn't interested in swallowing the bite of delicious food in his mouth. He did so, of course, with complete decorum. As always.

Impeccable manners were another of the things he really liked about himself. Plus, chewing and swallowing gave him a chance to replay their conversation.

Contemplate what was going on.

Lillie's big-eyed gaze settled on him. He tossed her a treat from his shirt pocket.

"Of course not. You've done nothing to offend me," he said when he could. Lifted his wineglass off the bench beside him and took a sip, to hide his own unease. Was it a lie to say she hadn't offended him when her *"seriously"* absolutely had done so? Technically, she'd said, not done it.

Though one could argue that saying was an act, and so had been done.

"Then what was that about? Me wanting to distance myself so that people didn't get the wrong idea? You're the one who invited me here today, Cole Bennet. Why do that if you were so worried about people drawing wrong conclusions about you?"

The question was a good one.

For which he had no stellar response. Other than the truth. "I'm not the least bit concerned about myself," he told her. His gaze more on her plate than anywhere else. "But you seem…kind of hesitant, meeting everyone, which made me think maybe you're shyer than I took you for and here I am throwing you into the middle of small-town life, with no idea if you've ever even lived in a small town. Or had any idea how the gossip mills work. Even the well-intentioned ones."

He felt her tense. Would like to have known what part of what he'd said had hit her hardest. Didn't figure they'd known each other long enough for the discussion a question on the matter might have raised.

But did venture out with, "Have you ever lived in a small town?"

"No. I grew up in Southern California, San Diego area."

A small town by Los Angeles standards, but definitely not anything close to the mere three thousand or so people who made up the year-round population of Shelter Valley. And maybe his first real piece of information about her actual life, not just her art.

"People in small towns tend to get up in each other's business," he said slowly, glancing around at the yard full of people he knew better than he knew his own parents. "Maybe more so here because we're so far from any other city. Don't get me wrong—it's not a mean-spirited thing at all. Quite the opposite. We're a close-knit group because we care about each other."

And that was kind of where his confessional came to a close.

"I thought it only fair to warn you that if we spend the entire afternoon hanging out, speculation will begin."

She'd taken a bite of broccoli salad. Tapped her fork in the air as she chewed. "And that bothers you," she said after swallowing.

"Not at all." He grinned. "All the attention kind of makes me feel famous...you know...as small towns go." When she glanced over at him, with a wry smile, he added, "You might just think you're eating lunch and making small talk with your new boss, but this town could have you married by nightfall..."

She laughed, as he'd meant her to. He chuckled, as well, just because the moment felt good.

"So, seriously, though, I don't want to lead anyone into thinking anything that isn't—"

"No worries," he cut her off. "If by anyone, you mean me, rest assured, I'm not reading anything more into our time together than a chief of personnel welcoming a new hire to town, and maybe—because you're surprisingly easy to spend time with, and mostly because Lillie likes you so much and is going to be nagging me to see you again—we become friends."

"I was actually more or less issuing a warning to myself." Her softly spoken words, followed by her setting her plate down, mostly untouched, on the bench, pulled the reins on his thoughts. Choking them right off.

"Mind explaining that?" he asked, setting his own plate aside. Gaining a Lillie glance from his uneaten meal to him.

"I'm in a whole new world here," she said on a very deep breath. "Facing challenges I've never faced."

Yeah, maybe saddling her with a new line had been a bit much for her first day on the job. Her talent more than warranted it. The hours she'd already agreed to work, helping with the other Christmas lines, allowed for the time commitment. But Lindsay, for all her natural ability and professional website, clearly wasn't used to success in her professional life.

"And I've never met anyone like you," she continued before he could figure out a way to make taking away the offer of her own line a positive thing. And then, for a second there, he just couldn't think at all.

*I've never met anyone like you.*

Guys like him didn't get lines like that.

"You make me laugh," she continued.

Okay, there. That he got. "I do tend to have that effect on women."

"No, I mean, inside, Cole. Where it can't be heard. Where it's felt."

He'd already suspected she'd been badly hurt in some way. Was pretty much positive at that point.

"I just… Who knows if my job here is going to work out, if I can do the work… I just don't want to lead—

"—everyone on, thinking that there's something between us when there isn't.

"I don't want to start something with you, no matter how right it feels, when I'm not in any position to make promises."

If it was possible for a guy who wasn't ever going to fall for a beautiful woman again to do so in the space of two lines, he might have just done so.

Luckily for him, such things didn't happen.

Not quite as much in his favor was the blank his mind was drawing when it came to any kind of response.

"And now I've said too much," she added, picking up her plate as she stood. "I'm an idiot, and sorry, and the whole work thing and how wrong it is for anyone in the workplace to…wow… I'm going to call a cab…"

He took hold of her elbow with only enough force to keep her from walking away if she didn't really want to do so.

"There is no cab service in Shelter Valley," he told her softly when she looked back at him.

Standing there, a look of extreme discomfort on her face, Lindsay shrugged. But not hard enough to pull away from him.

"If you wouldn't mind, it might be best if you sat back down," he told her with a bit of a grin. "Or the entire town will have us in our first lover's spat by nightfall."

Not true. Shelter Valley's citizens weren't that intrusive.

When she sat, words poured out of Cole of their own volition. "You haven't said too much, Lindsay. What you said was probably one of the nicest things anyone has ever said to me. And you have my word, I absolutely will not read more than friendship into any time we mutually decide to spend together."

When Lillie laid her head on Lindsay's knee, Cole might have smiled. If not for the seriousness of the conversation he wasn't done having. "Because as out of character as it is for me, I find myself thinking it feels right to spend time with you, too."

Her glance was long and intrusive. He had no problem whatsoever withstanding it.

"You're my boss."

"Only at work," he told her. "And not really, because you're contracted help. You're your boss. I'm, or rather Elite Paper, is your client. That aside, though, in a town the size of this one, if, outside the workplace, people couldn't associate on a personal level with people with whom they worked, then…we'd all have to walk around ignoring one another."

Her grin lit up her face. And his spirits.

"Then I'm glad we're in a small town," she told him, and dug into her salads.

## Chapter Six

Lindsay ate a lot of salads that next week. She flew through her days on a freedom high as she designed, without any of her usual plethora of back-to-back meetings and business meals. Her normally ringing-off-the-hook phone was mostly silent.

At home, Lindsay Warren-Smythe thrived on the busyness of a schedule that kept her mentally challenged from the time she got up in the morning until she went to bed at night. Gourmet food was served up to six times a day, depending on how many meal functions she had to attend.

In Shelter Valley, she had to seek out sustenance. Turned out, Ms. Bohemian was most fond of salads. Every variety. And she liked to be outdoors, taking long walks by the mountain and through town, too. The latter could just be a result of the very small living space within which she had to contain herself.

She didn't see her father. But she did what she was really there to do—get to know him—through others. Apparently a person couldn't work at Elite Paper without hearing songs of praise for Brent Wilson. It seemed to Lindsay that everyone she met had a founding-father story.

All good. The man worked in the trenches. He offered fabulous employee benefits, donated to the community—and to some personally when they were in need. He had a great sense of humor, had even played a practical joke or two along the way. And if someone was in need, he always made time to listen.

Too good to be true, in Lindsay's opinion. No one was that perfect, as she told Savannah in their almost nightly phone calls.

Yet, she listened to every story. Every comment. Played them back in her mind as she lay in bed at night. Telling herself her avid attention to any Wilson detail was borne out of justifying her presence in Shelter Valley.

And the salads, they were just for her.

Though Cole had taken up her pleasure quest in that area, finding bizarre, new, different or specialty salads in the Phoenix valley for her to try.

The day of the barbecue at the Wilson home, she'd opted to stay outside with Lillie and visit with townspeople while Cole went in to help the Wilsons put food away before the cleaning crew came in.

And on the way home, when he'd invited her to join him and Brent for lunch the following day, she'd politely declined. Automatically, before she'd given the matter a second's thought. With Lillie nosing her neck, she'd calmly come out with a set of guidelines by which she and Cole could spend time together as friends. No forethought on that, either. The rules had just been there.

They wouldn't hang out in Shelter Valley where townspeople would see them and make more of their relationship than was there. And they wouldn't socialize with work people, or talk about work, when they were together after hours, so there was no sense of impropriety.

No talk of work meant no conversation involving Brent Wilson, which meant that if it ever came out that she was Brent's daughter, Cole would know that she hadn't been using him. If he was just chief of personnel for Elite Paper, it wouldn't have mattered, but as a friend…both versions of Lindsay had to have his back.

As to whether or not she was going to tell Brent Wilson he was her father, she was leaning more toward a no. But hadn't fully reached the conclusion as of that following Saturday as she and Cole, with Lillie in the backseat, returned from an afternoon of chaperoning the dog for visits at one of the nation's top fifty children's hospitals.

"You're really good with those kids," Lindsay told Cole as he headed out of the city for the hour drive back to Shelter Valley. His shrug, so massive in his short-sleeved shirt, had her looking at him differently.

Not as a friend.

Or even someone for whom she had the secret and increasingly more potent hots.

But as a thirty-one-year-old man who would make a great father and was of an age to be getting on that. The way he'd knelt—his knees left bare by the shorts he wore, unprotected on the hard floor—with a five-year-old child who'd wanted to pet Lillie, but had been afraid. A minute or two with Cole there, and the little girl was giggling as Lillie's tongue made a quick swipe at the girl's chin.

"I'm surprised you aren't already married with a houseful of them," she said then, more curious than circumspect. More Warren than Warren-Smythe.

Another shrug was her only response.

Like he was hiding something. Would rather not talk about the entire marriage-and-kids subject. Because he'd been hurt? Had a fiancée who'd been killed, maybe? No other reason she could think of that a woman wouldn't want to marry the man.

Or…

Horrified, she stared at him…remembering the previous weekend when she'd alluded to the fact that she was attracted to him. "Are you gay?" she asked, kindly. Feeling stupid, inept, and wanting only to give him full support. Didn't mean, in any way, that he couldn't have kids, but maybe he struggled to come out in his small town.

"No."

The tone of his response, just that one word, left absolutely no doubt that the man was straight.

His expression, the odd disappointment in the glance he gave her, surprised her.

She'd slammed shut the door she'd kind of opened—

telling him that she had feelings for him, in terms of starting something between them—the second after she'd opened it. By insisting on friendship only.

"I'm just…you're the whole package, Cole. Aware, fair, sensitive to the feelings of others, strong, kind, a compassionate leader, fun and funny and way too hot for my good." The words poured out of Ms. Bohemian in a frantic attempt to undo any damage she'd done to her new friend. "I find it hard to believe that you aren't taken," she finished lamely, feeling Lillie's eyes on her, whether they actually were or not. The girl was in the middle seat behind her. Last time Lindsay had glanced back, Lillie had been watching out the front windshield. She didn't check to see if that was still the case.

Didn't want to feel the full throttle of the collie's disapproval.

Because one thing was for certain, as much as Lillie tended to everyone around her, most particularly gravitating to those experiencing emotional upheaval, Cole was always the dog's first and foremost person. She only tended to others when she knew he was set.

Cole's head shake drew her thoughts from the girl in the backseat. "I wouldn't have thought you'd be one to pander," he said with a small chuckle.

"Pander?" She wasn't one to get angry easily, or to give in to the emotion when it hit, but there it was, spreading under her skin. Making her face hot.

With a brief glance in her direction, showing her his creased brows and self-deprecating look, Cole set the cruise control and settled back in his seat as he said, "Way too hot for your good? You don't think that's just a tad bit overkill? If a tad meant total?" He shook his head with another disbelieving chuckle.

"Well, I'm not feeling all that hot for you right now," she said, with a huff as she smoothed her long, lightly flowing red paisley skirt down her ankles as though the world depended on getting it just right. Telling herself to let the conversation die. But couldn't do it. "I don't lie, Cole." She skated thin ice, though, apparently. Since the advent of her father into her life. And had to go on a cruise before she returned home, even if just a short day trip to Catalina Island because she'd told everyone in her real life that that's what she was doing during her leave.

"You have the hots for me." He shook his head again. Staring straight ahead.

"Yes." She might as well have added the "so there" that her tone of voice implied. And then, filled with defensiveness, added, "Have you looked at you?"

"Every day. I'm the guy women are friends with, and I'm good with that. I don't need you to pretend otherwise. Truth be known, I'm rather disappointed that you thought you had to." How a voice could be filled with so much confidence, when issuing those words, she didn't know.

She didn't get it, either. Cole wasn't male model gorgeous. He was so much more than that.

"I didn't think I had to do anything where you and your looks are concerned," she said, segueing as far away from her own exposure as she could, seeing that she hadn't meant to say out loud that she'd been spending way too much time thinking about going to bed with her new friend. "But now I'm wondering what on earth gave you the idea that I wouldn't find you attractive."

"Seriously? We're going to do this?" He glanced her way, shook his head briefly, and, not only had he thrown her own "seriously" comment back at her from the week before, but she thought she saw a grin on his face, too.

What the hell!

"Okay, let's go then," he said when she remained silent. "You're a beautiful woman. From the time I was in junior high, I've had the phone numbers of more beautiful women than I can count. And they were calling me—it wasn't me calling them. To talk about their love lives. With other guys."

"Yeah," she said, when he seemed to think he'd said enough. "You're sensitive to how people feel. It's a given they'd come to someone who'd understand. But also, you were someone who was a member of the opposite side, so could, by nature of that, offer actual counseling, not just sympathy."

She was speaking as a friend. And not as the beautiful woman he'd called her.

"Did you ever think about, maybe, calling someone and asking her out?" Not *her* her, not Lindsay, but… maybe Lindsay. If things with her father took a miraculous turn and she'd actually be visiting Shelter Valley now and then when her leave of absence from Warren-Smythe's life was over, it could happen.

Now she was pandering. To herself.

"Hundreds of times."

"Did you actually do it?" She couldn't take her eyes off him.

"Yes." He was grinning. Which made her stomach drop in the way it did when she wanted her body to know his body better.

"And?"

"We ended up as friends."

"Then you know the wrong women."

His shrug seemed easy. As did the glance he sent her. "I actually like who I am," he told her. "I love my life."

The truth rang so strongly in his words, she didn't know what to say to that. She certainly couldn't apply those same words to herself.

Proven by the fact that she was there, knowing him.

"You really expect me to believe you've never been in a long-term intimate relationship?" The bohemian was going to have to be reined in sooner, rather than later.

"I didn't say that."

That news made her heart take a dive. Which made no sense at all when she was busy convincing him he could have any woman he wanted.

"You were in one?" She had to verify. Just to keep the facts straight.

"I was engaged."

*Was.*

"What happened?" Best to know the details before envying the unknown female. Or…horror struck…*had* she died? And Cole's heart was forever taken?

"Engagement photos, newspaper announcement, wedding plans. Registered for gifts, sent invitations, church booked, tux purchased, rehearsal dinner, wedding morning rush, guests arrived, and I walked in and stood, watching the bridal party come up the aisle, waiting for my bride to appear."

He shrugged. Shook his head. Sent her a grin.

And stopped talking.

"She didn't appear?" Horrified, she stared at him. Glanced back at Lillie, as though the dog would give her some clue as to what to do next. Lillie was watching out the front windshield.

"Nope." With a sideways head tilt he added, "She was there, but instead of heading up the aisle, she ran out the side door. I found her, five minutes later, sitting in a pool of white satin and lace on a swing on the church playground, crying her eyes out."

Enthralled, in a horror movie kind of way, she asked, "What did you do?" Seeing a road sign that let her know they were already halfway back to Shelter Valley, she quickly returned her gaze to Cole. Didn't want their time together that day to end so soon. Wasn't ready to be done with him until the next time.

"I listened to her, of course. And then counseled her to change her clothes, hold her head high and get out there and find the life that was waiting for her." She stared at him. From his easy expression, the lack of tension in his face or neck, the nonchalant way he held the wheel with one hand…he really was as fine about it all as he sounded.

"You told her to leave you?"

"She loved me—she just wasn't in love with me."

"So why did she agree to marry you?"

"She didn't want to lose me."

Oh.

"Thing was, I understood. I didn't want to lose her. And with a little time putting things into perspective, I realized I wasn't in love with her, either. I loved her. And I was in love with the marriage and family part of it."

"How much time did it take you to get to that realization?"

"Thirteen days."

"You counted the days?"

With another grin, a huge one, he reached a hand over his shoulder, and patted the head that was instantly there, as though Lillie knew he'd been calling to her.

"No, I adopted Lillie thirteen days later and that night—with a six pack of beer for me, and the timed medications for her—I was telling her my sad life story when the truth came tumbling out."

He chuckled. Lillie nosed him in the shoulder.

And, choking back tears, Lindsay laughed.

Still in a flux over Lindsay's sudden "hots" confession, Cole was glad to turn the heat in an entirely different direction. Even if it put him on the hot seat.

He was glad to hear her laugh. Laughter, he was good at. Creating it. And living with it.

A gorgeous woman having the hots for him, not so much. He could handle the assuaging of the heat just fine, if it ever came to that. Had no doubts about his prowess in that area. Nicky had told him more than once that he was her best sex, ever. Not since Josh was in the picture, of course.

Because neither of them had talked about it.

No, it wasn't the fact that Lindsay Warren found

herself attracted to him that was the problem. It was the rest of it.

His falling in love with the idea of marriage and kids, and her falling in love with being his friend, were the concerns. He'd lived through the humiliation of being left at the altar once.

It wasn't happening again.

And so, because Lindsay seemed entertained by the Nicky story, he continued on with it as he got them back to Shelter Valley. Telling her about his recent invitation to be godfather to Nicky's soon to be born son.

"You're what now?" she asked, staring at him.

Because he'd had the same reaction, he grinned at her. "I know, kind of weird, right? But she's my best friend, I'm hers, so…there you go."

The sudden flash of disappointment he thought he saw on Lindsay's face before he had to get his gaze back to the road hit him hard enough that he couldn't let it go.

Wondered what it meant.

Why mention of a best friend would upset her.

And added the unanswered question to the pile of them that had been accumulating in the nine days he'd known her.

"You want to come home with us for dinner?" He asked a question for which he was certain he'd at least get an answer, even if it was a negative one, as he pulled off the highway and onto the ramp that would lead them back into town.

"What are you having?"

"We can stop at the deli and I'll run in and get a sampling of every salad they have in the case, and do a taste test if you want." Ideas just seemed to flow when she was around.

"You're on." Lindsay was smiling again, for real, petting Lillie again, too, as he pulled up out front of the Shelter Valley Deli. Leaving the car running for the air conditioning the females inside would need, he headed inside. Filled with more anticipation than was good for him.

Lindsay saying she had the hots for him aside, the woman was calling to him in a way that concerned him. Like when a human resources employee had found out her husband, who also worked at Elite Paper—in the manufacturing plant—had been having an affair with a dancer in Phoenix. Professionally, Cole hadn't been able to do anything about that. Being a disrespectful jerk of a husband wasn't reason enough to fire someone. But he'd helped the woman out with extra vacation days when she'd needed time off to move into her own place and get through the divorce.

Something was going on with Lindsay Warren. The obvious conclusion was that she was running from something.

He wanted to be there for her.

To have her trust him enough to confide in him so that he *could* help.

In all honesty, he wanted to assuage her hot situation, too.

Beyond that, he just wanted.

And that did not please him at all.

## Chapter Seven

Lindsay had never met a man more comfortable in his own skin. Nor had she known how much of a turn-on that was. Cole had manners and decorum, but they didn't seem to rule him, as such traits did in the society in which she'd grown up.

He burped once after dinner, clearly a surprise to him as he opened his mouth to speak and the sound of rushed air came out. Instead of hiding behind his hand, bowing his head, quietly excusing himself, he laughed. And said, "Well, there you have it, my table manners at their best, and in other news, excuse me."

She laughed out loud. At the sound. Burps were funny, why not just admit that and accept them as a part of life?

And she laughed at him, too. The words, the tone of his voice, the look on his face, the infectious smile…

And in her own other table news, she passed the taste test, naming all but one of the salads he fed her, a forkful at a time.

He won the contest, though, when she insisted on feeding him, too. She mixed two salads together, thinking she'd trip him up, but he was onto her just from the scent.

Told her so before she got the fork through his lips.

Which stopped her forward progress for the second it took her to stare at the open lips so close to hers. His teeth were perfect, white and straight, and that tongue—strong and lean—looked as though it could pleasure a woman's parts in any way she'd ever want...

His mouth came closer to the fork she held. Eyes closed, he wouldn't have known where...she glanced up, saw him watching her, and the fork in her hand started to shake.

Cole's mouth continued coming closer. Her fork moved to the side. His lips didn't follow it. They were heading closer to her, as were the eyes gazing into her own.

Frozen in place, melting inside, she waited.

The first touch changed her. His lips, soft, but firm, gently coaxed hers, and they fell to his power. Wanting to go wherever he went. Open, closed, hungry, holding back. She took and she gave it all. His knees touched hers, as they sat facing each other on the stools at his kitchen bar. Their lips did more than touch.

His tongue entered her mouth as though it belonged there, knew where to go and how to make her want more.

And she answered with a moan that escaped before she'd been aware it was coming.

Hungrier than she'd ever been in her life, she pressed her lips harder against his, needing her breasts pressed up against his chest and...

A wet push against the underside of her hand knocked the potato-and-bean-salad-filled fork. She heard it hit the floor. Pulled back.

And stared into the big brown eyes looking up at her with wisdom. Knowing. And a refusal to allow her to ignore either.

"Well, there you go," she said, breathless. Slipping off the stool, she reached for the fork. Watched as Lillie cleaned up the mess.

And saw Cole's thighs as he vacated his stool and moved over to the sink.

"I'm not going to apologize," he said, rinsing the fork he'd taken from her mostly numb fingers.

"I know." She wasn't, either.

"Good, that's all cleared up then."

The salad mess she'd made? The apology issue? Or the kiss itself?

Afraid of the answer, of where it could lead, Lindsay left well enough alone.

Cole told himself not to notice the hardness of Lindsay's nipples through the tight short-sleeved white top she had on. Or to catalog the news that she wasn't a padded bra woman.

He did both, anyway. Stood by the sink, running cold water over a very clean fork, until he could round the corner without his hard-on being as obvious as her breasts.

He thought about burping again just to change the mood, but couldn't get enough air sucked into his lungs to make it happen. She took care of the immediate problem for both of them, moving away from the kitchen to look at the collage of pictures he'd scattered over the wall in the adjoining family room.

When Lillie didn't follow their guest, but rather sat staring at him, he knew he was in more trouble than he'd thought.

Patting her head, he tossed her a treat, and a silent you did good nod, knowing that she'd broken up the kiss on purpose. She'd obviously sensed his emotional upheaval.

At least that was the theory he was choosing to adopt. Could be the girl had just been going for the salad that had lowered to within grasp of her mouth.

"Wait," Lindsay said, staring at a small black-framed photo, similar to about twenty others along the wall. "You went to the Sandra Day O'Connor College of Law?"

Arizona State University's law school in Phoenix, though she might not know that. He'd forgotten the photo was up there.

He nodded. Sipped from the one bottle of beer he was allowing himself before he drove her home.

She shook her head. Stared at him. "And then, what, you just didn't take the bar exam?"

"I took it."

"No way you didn't pass."

He smiled at that. Couldn't help himself. Passing the bar was no easy feat. Classmates he'd expected to breeze through much more easily than him had failed the first time.

"I passed."

"You're a lawyer?" Her voice almost squeaked with surprise.

He shrugged. Nodded. Sipped.

"And…that's Brent Wilson in the graduation photo with you?" That question held emotion. Not surprise. And not anything that sounded good. Though why she'd be dismayed that his boss had attended his law school graduation, he had no idea. "I thought you'd gotten to know him because you work for him…"

Why it should matter to her, he didn't know, but paid attention to the fact that it did. She'd said no work talk. Didn't want any hint of impropriety.

Was she afraid he was a spy for his boss? More in with the man at the top than he'd led on? That he'd kiss and tell?

Didn't make a lot of sense given the fact that he'd be tattling on himself as well.

"He treats you like family… Lillie thinks his house is her second home…you help him serve at his parties… are you related to him?"

The look on her face was definitely not pleasure.

More like horror, though he was fairly certain his normal intuitive senses were on the fritz at the moment. Given their recent…encounter.

Obviously hers were, too. A part of him gloated for

a second over that realization. The rest of him kind of panicked. He had to get it all shut down.

Immediately.

"No, I'm not related to him." He started with the easiest, most obvious answer. And was surprised to see the immediate softening of her features.

Relieved was more like it. They were both on overload. Just needed a minute or two to recover equilibrium. If he'd been talking to a friend who'd come to him about her reactions to being kissed, he'd have known instantly that the ensuing reactions would be subject to error. Would have counseled her to relax. To not overreact.

Lindsay was still looking at the photo.

"My parents moved to Shelter Valley when I was ten," he told her. "They were both stationed at the air force base in West Phoenix and had decided, because of my lack of fitting in due to all the moving around and my overly large size, that I needed a more stable home life. With both of them being colonels at that point, their travel obligations were less. And then one thing led to another, promotions, different responsibilities that were good for their careers meant that they were both on deployment a lot more. Brent and Emily had become friends with them, and they watched over me whenever my mom and dad were both gone at the same time. I was sixteen by then, fine on my own, but Brent made me his personal business."

"So you gave up law practice to pay him back?" She seemed to find something distasteful about that.

"No. I keep my license current, and my education,

too, and use my law degree to counsel employees, and Brent, in terms of law changes and best practices in personnel situations. And, when asked, I strategize with Elite's full-time business lawyer. I'm the one who chose to work for Elite. Brent fought me all the way, wanting me to take a partnership position I'd been offered at a prominent Phoenix firm. The law interests me. Fighting, defending, prosecuting, making deals, does not. Brent is all about the people, the quality of the workplace and of the product. The man's a genius when it comes to earning. He just spends more on quality than most would. And that's the kind of world I want to work in."

The shell-shocked look on her face told him he'd gone a little too far in his defense of his mentor and boss. Had been too intense in his delivery.

And so he took a deep breath, cringed inside and burped.

The second Lindsay was back at home after dinner—a chaperoned drop-off with Lillie ready to jump into the front seat as soon as Lindsay vacated—she was on the phone with Savannah.

"Find me some flaws. I don't care how much it costs."

"Excuse me?"

Pacing the apartment, from bedroom through living room to kitchen and back, Lindsay stared at the bare feet visible beneath the hem of her skirt. "Brent Wilson. It's too clean. Too perfect. No one's perfect."

"What's going on, Lins?"

"If I take at face value everything I'm hearing, the man's a saint. And I know firsthand that he is not.

I'm here to find out why he deserted my mother and me, or at least to find some kind of closure where he's concerned, and all this praise isn't getting me there." Through the living room, back to the bedroom and turn. Ms. Bohemian needed to make enough to afford a bigger place. Or, at the very least, a balcony where one could get some fresh air.

"I thought you were there to get to know him. Find out who he is."

"Which is what I just said." Her frustration level settled down a notch as she heard her tone of voice. And did a mental replay of her exact words to her friend. *I'm here to find out why he deserted my mother and me.* Not once had she stated that intention aloud.

She was flailing around like a hooked fish. She'd not only kissed Cole, she'd have gone to bed with him if he'd asked. Cole, who was her father's mentee.

"After all these years, I'm thinking the only way you're going to get answers to a decision a man made nearly twenty-nine years ago, give or take a month, is to ask him."

"I can't do that." Technically, she could form the words in his presence. She wasn't going to. She'd decided that before she'd had Savannah put the current plan in motion. Most likely, the answer would be a lie. He wasn't going to tell her to her face that he'd had better things to do than raise a daughter.

"You knew that going in."

Right. She'd come to town to surreptitiously get to know the man. Because it had seemed like fate when Savannah's team had happened upon the job opening at Elite that seemed like it had been designed specifically for Lindsay Warren.

"It made more sense on paper," she said then, plopping down on the couch in the near dark, tucking her feet up under her skirt.

"Life events shape people." Savannah's words came softly. "It's possible that getting your mother pregnant, and then running out before you were born, turned Wilson's life around."

The idea didn't sit well with her. And yet...it kind of did. Her mother's addiction issues couldn't be laid completely at Wilson's feet. It wasn't like he forced her to take drugs. Lindsay didn't even know if he'd ever taken them with her. And her own life...she'd done just fine without him.

So if her growing up without him meant that he was a great father, provider, business owner, benefitting the lives of so many others...

"It's all too perfect," she said again. "No one's perfect."

Perfect. Perfect. Perfect.

She strived for perfection in her art. In her life's work as chief fundraising officer. In her own personal behavior.

Did she expect it from others, too?

"Everyone has flaws," she said aloud, thinking maybe she'd just stumbled onto one of her own. Something to keep in mind.

Worry about later.

"You want us to dig deeper, we will."

"I do." And didn't feel a bit of shame, or guilt, about

that one. "As it stands, there's no way I can consider introducing myself to him. I won't implode the life he's built, bring scandal upon this town or hurt the hundreds of people who look up to him, who rely on him, if he's for real."

"We knew that going in, too."

Samantha's softly uttered response didn't ease the tension in Lindsay. If anything, the confirmation worsened her own inner battle.

Because if she couldn't come clean about her identity in Shelter Valley, she couldn't entertain even the slightest hope of a possibility that she and Cole Bennet could be anything more than short-term friends.

Cole told himself a lot of things. For the remainder of Saturday night, into Sunday morning, he laid down mandates. Mostly to do with cooling down relations with Lindsay Warren.

He kept them, too, throughout the day. The fact that he had back-to-back obligations made his task somewhat more doable. Starting with an early morning basketball game followed by breakfast and a shower before church, he stayed on track. Then a nine-hole game of golf with a couple of buddies from high school and a promise to show up at Homestead Ranch to watch Brent's thirteen-year-old daughter, Kaitlin, practice her barrel jumping for an upcoming rodeo kept him out of trouble for most of the afternoon.

Right up until he'd climbed into his SUV with several hours of sunlight shining ahead of him. And the specter of running into Lindsay at the office the next morning with that kiss hanging there between them. If it was awkward, others would notice.

He absolutely didn't want her to get cagey and leave. At all. Most certainly on Elite Paper's behalf. Her talent was looking to be the year's greatest asset.

And for himself…well, he hadn't enjoyed being with anyone as much as her. Not in way too long, at any rate.

Yet, he couldn't really say he knew her. In all of the dinners and drives and time they'd spent together over the previous many days, she'd mentioned nothing personal about her life.

He knew she liked wine, but could only handle a couple of glasses before she fell asleep. That she adored salads. That she was a gifted artist who only sold her wares online and at the shows listed on her website.

That she was from Southern California—San Diego.

She'd never had a dog, but seemed as taken with Lillie as the old girl was with Lindsay.

That she drove an old car, that her apartment was the smallest one available in Shelter Valley and that it was pretty much barren inside. No wall of photos like he'd hung in his family room, that was for sure. From what he'd seen at a brief glimpse on the way from the bathroom the one time he'd been up to her place to help her carry in the bags of veggies she'd picked up at a fresh market in Phoenix, there hadn't been a single piece of decor even in her bedroom.

Her parents, past relationships—hell, maybe even a current one—her education or dreams or goals…all a blank.

In the many hours they'd spent together, she'd never

offered a thing about herself. And he hadn't wanted to push. Used to women spilling their guts to him, he'd never had to do so.

But what if she was hiding something? Running from someone?

His way wasn't to run from things.

The reminder drove him to push his vehicle's hands-free system, call her and ask if she wanted to visit Yu-cacho Peak—a popular viewpoint a quarter of the way to Phoenix—with him. With the heat reaching a hundred and fifteen that afternoon, they'd have no trouble securing a little table on the covered and misted portion of the cemented overlook. He'd bring a fresh fruit salad and bottles of ice water.

He felt a twinge of guilt at her ready acceptance.

Because of the rush of hormonal pleasure shooting through him.

A sensation that hit again as he pulled on the light-weight shorts and loose-fitting tank with tennis shoes and, telling Lillie he'd be back before bedtime, headed back out the door before the girl could make her opinion on his state known to him.

His attire exposed impressive shoulders and arm muscles. His reason for wearing it was the fifteen-minute paved walk he'd be taking with Lindsay after they united in the peak's parking lot.

Her suggestion that they drive separately had been a good one, he'd decided. Kept distance between them.

Realizing that the choice meant she'd probably been having issues over that kiss too, that like him she needed to make sure that nothing came of it, didn't please him as much as it should have done.

No worries, though. The walk up to the peak in triple-digit temps would tax both of them. The cooler he'd be hauling, and the extra ten pounds he always carried, would hopefully leave him pleasantly tired out.

He had it all figured out. Thought the plan as perfect as it could get. Right up until Lindsay got out of her snazzy little old yellow car wearing black Lycra bike shorts that pretty much showed him what she'd look like naked, and a red-white-and-blue tie-dyed cropped spaghetti-strap T-shirt that covered her waistband— just barely.

Before she'd even reached him, Cole had the cooler that had been hoisted on his shoulder down, unzipped, had a bottle of water out, uncapped, and was sucking it down as though to save his life.

## Chapter Eight

Lindsay was glad to see Cole. The part where her heart sped up and she got all squirrely down below, she ignored. His grin as he greeted her, water bottle still at his lips, brought a ready smile to her own lips.

Being with him just plain did that to her.

And short-term friends aside, she had questions to ask of him. Not about Brent Wilson. The man was most definitely off-limits as far as conversation with Cole Bennet was concerned. After his revelations from the night before—his mentor-like attachment to the man Lindsay did not trust—she couldn't listen to another sentence Cole had to say about her father.

Had already heard too much.

No way was she going to risk Cole ever thinking that she'd been using him to get to her father. The hiring interview, okay, on a stretch, yeah maybe. Although it hadn't been Cole she'd been using, but rather her father's chief of personnel.

She'd been so careful not to allow any talk of work, and thus Brent Wilson, into any of their conversation since the day of the barbecue. And then she'd seen that picture on Cole's wall—the law degree Cole had been holding open to the camera—and Ms. Bohemian, who'd still been swirling from the kiss, had started blurting words.

But the questions she did have for him...

"I heard that there's a horse therapy program, mainly for kids, being run at a place called Homestead Ranch here in town," she said as soon as they fell into step on the paved walkway leading up the mountain.

Savannah had told her about the program the night before, after Lindsay—who'd been looking for distraction from thoughts of Cole and needing something else to do when she was in town and not working—had mentioned wanting to do some small-time fundraising for therapy dog programs in Phoenix.

Nothing on the scale she'd do once she got back home. But if she was going to complete her mission without anyone getting hurt, she had to get Lindsay Warren-Smythe back on the front page before Ms. Bohemian created a mess she couldn't fix.

Warren-Smythe wouldn't be there in any formal way, of course, or her cover would be completely blown. And chances were really good that if that happened, Brent Wilson would be exposed, even if just between the two of them. He'd impregnated a Warren-Smythe. Not too many of those hanging around. Most particularly not female ones who were twenty-eight.

Cole had stepped to the side to allow an older couple coming down the path to pass them, with Lindsay waiting just down from him, her back also against the mountain wall.

"I was just at Homestead this afternoon," he told her as they resumed their walk. "The owner, Mia Jones, is a friend of mine. We went to high school together."

Oh. Well, good. She had an in then. Because as she and Savannah had both determined the night before, she couldn't use the Sierra's Web connection, which was how Savannah even knew about the program.

And Cole spending the afternoon with a woman friend, this Mia Jones, should not in any way diminish her pleasure in the day.

Short-term friends had absolutely no ownership of any committed feelings such a jealousy.

"You and Mia an item then?" Ms. Bohemian spilled the words. "I hope the time we've spent together this past week, while you're being so nice and making me feel welcome, doesn't bother her?"

He seemed to miss a step. But then she saw the jutted part of mountain wall that interrupted the path they were on. Made sure she stepped over it as he said, "Hardly. Mia's a one-guy woman, and when the one guy broke her heart their senior year at Montford, there was no hope for anyone else. I talked her into giving herself a chance to fall in love again when she met a pretty dynamic guy through her brother. She gave it her best shot, the new guy wanted to marry her, but her heart just wasn't in it. Instead, she took her father's failing farm and turned it into a huge financial success."

"Wow." Lindsay felt a sudden kinship with the woman. Not the boyfriend breaking her heart part, but the brokenness inside that kept one focused on things that one could control.

"What happened to the second guy?"

"He was offered a professorship at Montford. They're still friends."

The idea pleased her. Gave her a seed of hope that somehow she and Cole could remain in contact. Until Warren-Smythe piped up silently, reminding her why that couldn't happen for them.

And they were right back to Mia being all alone and Cole spending Sunday afternoon with her. "You help her out then?" She asked, figuring, great guy that he was, he'd handle heavy work for a friend who asked.

"I have in the past on occasion," he said, rounding another curve on their way to the top. Revealing an already glorious view of the world extending as far as the eye could see. "But she's got all the help she needs now," Cole continued. "Crazy story, but it turns out that she and her first love, Jordon, had donated embryos to some couple whose stuff wasn't compatible. They froze them and the woman had twins four years ago. The couple was killed in a boating accident and left the twins to Jordon. He showed up in town last month, completely shell-shocked with these two little girls in tow."

Cole was grinning, and she was, too. She couldn't help it. The way he had of relaying information—it all came alive in the best possible way.

"So...she got the kids?" Savannah had said that Kelly and Mariah, who Lindsay knew to be the psychiatrist and child life expert partners in Sierra's Web, had worked with Mia. She hadn't been able to disclose why. Lindsay had assumed it had to do with horse therapy. That the three had shared a young client...

"The kids and the guy," Cole told her. "Turns out, he'd been as unsuccessful as she'd been at finding anyone else to fill his heart. So now you've got these two businesspeople, both single through their twenties, trying to keep up with two very busy and determined four-year-olds. It's a hoot to watch." His chuckle as he told her about the twins calling their biological mother Mama Mia and singing a song from the popular musical to her the first week they met her had Lindsay smiling, and tearing up.

Cole not only brought his stories more alive, but apparently their listeners, too.

Something Lindsay would be prudent to remember.

And guard against.

Damn. She'd done it again. Gotten him talking, seeming so interested and entertained by his conversation that he just went blithely on, and failed to get any return out of her.

Determined not to go home without at least one new piece of personal information about Lindsay Warren, Cole went back to her original question.

"What's your interest in horse therapy?" he asked, as they drew closer to the top of the smallish mountain they were ascending. Had she been in therapy herself?

Or did she know of someone who could benefit from it? A child maybe?

Had she had a child? Lost custody of it somehow?

Or was there a younger sibling, maybe a troubled one, still back in California?

He was sweating, but not dripping with it. Poured a bit of water left in the bottom of his bottle down his shoulders, just in case, as he awaited her answer.

"I'm interested in pet therapy in general," she told him, her tone as easy as it had been throughout their visits during the past week. "Until Lillie, I've never actually been exposed to it. And horse therapy, I looked it up last night…it's fascinating. Did you know in Arizona that there are wild horses that, when hurt, are rescued, and then many of them find homes as therapy horses?"

"I did know that," he said, with a nod. And a quick sideways grin at her.

"Of course you did. You know Mia." She grimaced. "Sorry. Anyway, I've done some fundraising…it's something I enjoy, and I thought maybe I could reach out to them, to Mia, Homestead, whoever and see if they'd like me to see what I can do. For free, of course. I just… It's a way I could…"

Cole's mood soared. Shelter Valley was already growing on Lindsay! She wanted to be a part of the community. His joy was for Elite Paper, he told himself.

Even as he knew that joke was on him.

"The horse therapy program, Forever Friends, is run by Mariah Montford," he told her.

"Didn't you say the vet you got Lillie from was named

Montford? And I met her and her husband at the bar-becue."

"Cassie, yes. Her husband, Sam, is the son of the town's founders. Sam met Mariah's parents in the Peace Corps. Her father was a Native American. The couple was killed by insurgents and had named Sam as her guardian. Mariah, who was five or six at the time, had witnessed the whole thing and for the first many months that Sam had her, Mariah didn't speak at all. Cassie's pet therapy program helped bring Mariah back to life."

"And now Mariah runs a horse therapy program," Lindsay said, nodding, and sounding...focused and supportive, too. In a practical business way he hadn't noticed in her before. Like she was already planning...

"I'm sure that she'd love to talk to you," he said next. "I can introduce you to her if you'd like." As a man who knew her from work and had heard about her interest. Not as someone personally interested in Lindsay Warren. A friendly gesture.

Because he was a friendly guy.

"That'd be great," Lindsay's tone, still uplifted, sounded more like the artist he'd like to know more about.

And want less.

The view from the top was magnificent. Even better than the glorious landscape visible from the path she'd taken in Shelter Valley. The colors, vivid blue sky, mountains and vegetation in a breathtaking panorama as far as she could see, all topped by sunshine that made everything glow like gold...a woman could almost believe that she could achieve everything her heart desired, could be anyone she wanted to be, sitting up there looking out at the world.

Munching on watermelon and grapes, cantaloupe, strawberries and bananas from the plastic dish Cole had set between them, Lindsay felt the misters' light touch and took a breath of pure happiness. And was struck by it. The uplifted excited sensation mixed with calm, the beauty and strength, the desire to remain in it…they were new to her. Or at least more potent than anything she'd ever known.

"You know my life story—what's yours?" Cole's question, floating on the air, sounding so easy and casual, hit her like a ton of landslide rocks.

She shook her head. At a complete loss for the second it took her to focus on real life again. "I grew up in Southern California. Lived in the same house until I was twenty, which was when I graduated from University of California San Diego and got my own place. And the rest you know. I'm an artist who makes enough to drive an old car, but one with character, mind you, and live in the smallest apartment in town." Her voice lightened as she got back into her groove, and she finished with a grin before popping a strawberry in her mouth.

Thus precluding any further awkward questions.

If she could just be Lindsay Warren-Smythe, who was always in the company of people who wanted things from her, knew her reputation for guarding her privacy and didn't want to offend her.

"My parents were colonels in the air force. What were yours?"

Cole only knew Ms. Bohemian. A fictional character residing in Warren-Smythe's body and who really probably needed to just get out.

"My dad is a businessman," she said. "And my mother's only career—stay-at-home mom." Truth. If perhaps misleading, since her mom had only stayed at home for a couple of months after Lindsay was born. After which she'd been moved to the cemetery.

A permanent home.

So, still true.

"Are your folks still here in Shelter Valley?" she asked then, realizing that he hadn't introduced her to them during Brent Wilson's barbecue. And figuring turnabout was not only fair play, but also would deflect the subject from her to him.

"Nope. They retired in Vermont. How about siblings?"

He shot the ball right back at her and suddenly that mountaintop, the lack of others willing to tackle the day's heat, seemed more of a cage than a symbol of freedom.

She couldn't think about the half siblings she'd read about, seen pictures of, but had never met. Might never meet.

"I grew up an only child," she told him. "Just like you." And it was time to move on. Standing, she continued with, "I'm getting warm—you mind if we head back down?"

She was warm. But pleasantly so.

Wasn't really ready to leave.

But she couldn't be a sitting duck. And couldn't afford any more of his questions, either. Not if she was going to keep her promise to herself not to lie to him.

Cole stood immediately as she put the lid on the bowl of fruit. He loaded up the few things he'd taken out of his backpack, hoisted the cooler and waited for her to lead the way down the path.

She wanted to believe she hadn't offended him, and she couldn't help but notice that he wasn't smiling.

Which had her in another quandary. Cole wasn't just another guy. He was one in a million. She should know. Over the years of fundraising, she felt like she'd met a million.

None of whom had opinions that had mattered to her like Cole Bennet's did. The whys and wherefores of that were something she could worry about another day. Or another hour later that day.

The man had just been trying to get to know her. The way of friendship, even short-term ones. In her panic about the possibility of being exposed, she'd overreacted. Searched her brain for things she could offer him that wouldn't give her up.

And came up with, "I never told my family, but I went skydiving when I was in college. The idea of jumping out of a plane just seemed so freeing, but I didn't want to worry anyone…" At a portion of the path where they could walk side by side, she slowed to wait for him to step up to her, and then continued walking, head bent to watch the ground for any pitfalls, and hoping that her words would bring back the smile to his face.

When he remained silent, she added, "This little hike…reminds me of it—except, you know, the whole feet on the ground thing." Don't babble, she reprimanded herself. Babblers gave themselves away every time.

"I've never even thought about jumping out of a plane," Cole interrupted her self-discipline tirade, his tone still a little off, then he added, "Which is probably a good thing for the parachutes of the world." His chuckle warmed her hugely. In the best way. Simply because it was back.

With a lighter step, she said, "I was scared, so it wasn't like the best feeling ever, but I still loved it. Being up here…it's like skydiving without the fear."

Had been like it. Until she'd panicked and ended their sweet moments alone at the top of the world. So typical of her.

And with him, more so than ever.

She didn't want to lose his friendship. Had no clue how to ensure that she didn't. They'd known each other less than two weeks. And already determined there'd never be anything serious between them.

So why did the fact that she was afraid she'd offended him feel so serious?

It was the kiss.

Typical.

Physical relations ruined things. They were messy and emotional and confusing and she wanted to kiss him again. Wanted to be kissed by him.

The trip down didn't take nearly as long as the trip up and they were back in the parking lot before Lindsay had found her zen. Cole wished her a good-night, got in his SUV, waited for her to drop down into her little yellow bomb and followed her out of the parking lot.

Without a single grin.

Or furthering his offer to introduce her to Mariah Montford. She could find the woman on her own now that she knew enough details about the horse therapy operation. It wasn't Cole's introduction to a town resident that bothered her.

It was his lack of any kind of smile as they parted.

For the rest of Sunday night, she occupied herself with fundraising research in Phoenix. Using her knowledge of what kind of venues to contact and what to present, to formulate a series of plans, and compile a list of calls to make the next day. All normal preliminary work that she wanted done before she approached Mariah Montford.

She'd been in her groove, zooming along as she did at home, from one business-related thought to the next, letting ideas flow, jotting them down and researching them as they presented themselves. Until, sometime around ten, she realized that her mind was almost frantically refusing to wind down. She had a full-time job that was expecting her best work in the morning. She had to get to bed.

And didn't want to lie there, in Cole's town, and think about having lost his smile.

He thought she'd blown him off. Or maybe that she was hiding something, which she was.

A hot bath and lavender bubbles and a glass of wine helped her get sleepy. The possibility that she'd been wrong about Cole, blowing things out of proportion, that maybe the hike had been too hot for him, that he'd be his usual self in the morning, allowed her to get a fair night's rest.

But the next morning, when a mailperson delivered an interoffice envelope to her desk, she had a sinking feeling.

Opening it in her own private little area, she turned her back to the door as she read the single sheet of paper.

Cole had sent her Mariah's contact information. No note. Not even a signature.

Standing, shaking inside more than out, she strode out of the art department and down the hall to the breezeway connecting the building's wings. If he wanted to be done with her, that was fine. Probably for the best.

But she was not going to let herself fade away without an apology. From the moment Savannah had called to tell her Sierra's Web had found her father, she'd promised herself that no one would get hurt by her very private, personal quest.

More than that, Cole had been burned enough.

She most definitely was not going to be the cause of him feeling as though he'd been left at the altar again. Or, as the case was, a picnic table in the sky.

She made it to the other side of the building without having to make conversation with anyone. Head down in the breezeway, staring at the blue jewels on her flip-flops beneath the long denim-and-silk-striped skirt, helped take care of any would-be conversationalists.

And the couple of business-attired individuals she passed in the hall on the way to Cole's office in the executive wing were seemingly preoccupied enough with their own business that she only had to smile and keep moving. A brief glance to the left showed her that Brent Wilson's door was closed at the end of the hall. Cole's door, to the right, was open.

In a short-sleeved white shirt and a tie, he was sitting behind his desk, seemingly engrossed in the large screen in front of him.

She walked in with a brief knock on the solid wood. Closed the door behind her as though she owned the building.

A Warren-Smythe move. Because generally, when she was visiting a personnel officer, she did own the building. At the moment, she was on autopilot. Needing the confidence it gave her.

"You have a minute?" she asked him, ignoring the fact that Lindsay Warren should have made an appointment. That she was going against the rule she'd set forth for their short-term friendship. The one that stipulated that at work, they were only boss and contracted employee.

A glance at the closed door, a raised eyebrow, let her know what he thought of her question. But he waved her to the chair in front of his desk.

With a generic kind look, minus any hint of a grin, and an equally bland, "What can I do for you?"

Panic struck. Warren-Smythe was no longer coming to the rescue. The twenty-eight-year-old had never been in a situation even a little like her current one.

She opened her mouth, ready to apologize, and Ms. Bohemian blurted out.

"Kiss me again."

## Chapter Nine

Cole straightened, back ramrod straight, as he frowned at the woman who'd just elegantly fallen into a seat across from him, her silky and denim skirt and form-fitting short-sleeved blue top there to torment him, he was sure.

Because that was the kind of mood he'd been in since the afternoon before.

It wasn't like him.

Lillie had made sure she was touching him in some way every second he'd been home. Other than his shower that morning and he was pretty certain she'd have joined him there if he'd have left the door open for her. As it was, she'd kept watch outside the door.

"What did you just say?" he asked Lindsay, knowing damned well the three words that had come clearly out of her mouth.

He just couldn't figure out why.

And couldn't pay attention to the hardness that had instantly sprung to life down below. He was not going to let his emotions turn traitor on him again. Nicky's lesson had been the last one he needed to learn on that subject.

"I'm sorry," she said, her shoulders back as she perched on the edge of the seat. "It's just… I wasn't putting you off, Cole, or rather, I was, but not because I was rejecting you, I just…"

"You have business to discuss?" he asked, fighting back a huge and completely inappropriate urge to grin.

She put an envelope on his desk. He recognized it by the black marker line across the subject box. He'd just had it delivered to her. "We said only business at work," she stated then, her tone firm again. "The information contained in this envelope has absolutely nothing to do with my Elite Paper employment, and therefore, should not have been inserted into a company envelope, nor sent through interoffice mail."

His lips twitched. He held them from the inside out, sucked up against his teeth.

He'd been letting her off the hook, sending the message that he wasn't going to bother her anymore. That she had nothing to fear from him in terms of pressuring her to give more of herself than she was comfortable giving.

Had been afraid that the kiss had made her feel uncomfortable.

*Kiss me again.*

Perhaps he'd read her all wrong.

If so, it was a first for him.

Her rebuff the day before had been clear. And he hadn't even touched her. He'd asked about her parents. About siblings. The most generic get-to-know-you queries.

And she'd put an abrupt end to their picnic. There weren't too many ways one could interpret those facts.

They clearly spelled hands off.

"I will, however, give you an opportunity to correct this egregious error if you would agree to see me after work tonight."

He had an afternoon golf tournament that was supposed to include happy hour and dinner with other businessmen in town as well as a dozen or so others from Phoenix.

"Where?"

"It's your town—you pick."

The whole thing was turning him on. Intriguing him. And pissing him off a little, too. Who did she think she was to get him all het up like she was? And them just being short-term friends.

For the time being.

Things changed all the time.

Raising his chin, he looked her straight in the eye. "My place."

She licked her lips. Tightened her chin. "For dinner," he added. He'd golf, stay for one drink and pick up steaks on the way home from the club.

"What about my car being seen in your driveway?"

"I'll pick you up."

"Fine."

She stood, that damned skirt—whoever heard of strips of silk and denim being sewn together—hugging her hips and tempting him to stand and kiss her just to get her back for having demanded that he do so.

He watched her walk to the door instead, noting how unusually straight she was still holding her spine. Felt a rush of compassion.

Along with a silent reminder that if she'd suffered some kind of trauma in her past, questions during a mountain picnic could have been hard to take.

"Hey, Lindsay?" he called out.

At the door she turned. "Yeah?"

"Did we just have our first fight?"

"It sure felt like it."

He nodded. It had felt like it to him, too. "You know this makes us officially friends now, right?"

Frowning, she half smiled as she looked at him. "How do you figure?"

"You like me." He grinned, hard and not caring.

"How do you figure?" she asked again with a scoff that seemed like an attempt to cover a smile.

"Because if you didn't you'd have just taken my note and called Mariah." His smile was huge at that point. He couldn't help it.

Lindsay Warren liked him.

And he liked her, too.

She'd had to make things right with Cole. The man was too special to think that she'd shunned him. He'd shared his insecurity with her—though she was sure he wouldn't call it that—and only a jerk would let him think that she was just one more in a line of women who didn't find him worthy of their sexual attention.

They shouldn't have kissed.

But her rebuff the night before had nothing to do with the fact that they had. Nor had it been any indicator of her desire for him, or lack thereof.

In retrospect, she'd figured out that that's what he'd thought. That she was another woman who liked talking to him, liked being friends, who just didn't see him as lover material.

While she finished work, went home and then waited for him to come pick her up for dinner, she made a very clear decision. If she did nothing else good in Shelter Valley, she was going to make certain that Cole Bennet gained a complete understanding of how very much a woman he considered beautiful wanted him.

The task she'd set herself was nearly impossible. She realized it even as she vowed to get the job done. How did she show him how valuable and perfect he was for her, without letting him even start to return the feelings?

How did she ensure that, when she had to leave, she wouldn't break his heart?

One word came to her. *Honesty.*

The thing she didn't have to give.

At least not in totality.

But if she was as honest as she could be? More open than she'd ever been with anyone else in her life?

Would that mean enough?

Since she didn't even know what the whole open thing meant, period, she could hardly determine what *enough* would look like.

Okay, so the plan wasn't clear yet.

But she had the goal.

One that met with full approval of all parts of herself.

An odd occurrence. One that made her smile. Just as Cole's smile had as she'd left his office. She wasn't off the hook. She'd hurt him the day before.

But he was giving her a second chance and she wasn't going to blow it.

Why she was getting so wrapped up in a person she'd know only briefly in her lifetime, she didn't know. Maybe because her emotional system was discombobulated with the whole scheme that had brought her to Shelter Valley.

The whys didn't seem to matter to Lindsay. Fact was, she was as driven to be friends with Cole Bennet as she had been to find her father. Whether the two forces were related, or just coincidence, she couldn't say.

Didn't particularly care at the moment.

She'd taken a leave from her life to resolve her inner conflicts and get on with the future. She had to trust herself. Couldn't control every nuance on the path.

So thinking, she walked boldly into Cole's home that night, following him in from the garage and then greeting Lillie as though she and the dog were good friends, rather than just friendly acquaintances.

"How was your day?" she asked the dog as she gave her a quick kiss on the neck and let her hand linger, scratching Lillie behind the ear.

"Better now that you're here," Cole answered, his tone almost baby talk as he spoke for the dog. Except the look in his eye seemed more personal than that.

As though he'd been answering for both of them?

Smiling at him, because she couldn't help it, Lindsay took the glass of wine he offered her, toasted it to the beer can he'd opened for himself and said, "My day's better, too."

She might not have all the answers, but she'd get this one right. She wasn't giving herself any other option.

Cole wanted to hope that Lindsay was sitting on his back patio, misters going, because there was something cool starting between them. He didn't let himself head off the rails that way. Instead, he was glad that they'd worked through their little bit of discomfort, swore to himself that he wouldn't touch her again and really hoped that she'd decide that she loved her job and wanted to stay in Shelter Valley.

The desire he did allow himself was that if she was hurting, as he suspected, or maybe even running from hurt, she'd trust him enough to let him help her through it. That was one of the things he was good at. Helping women who were in emotional turmoil find their way out. He liked that about himself.

He'd kissed her. And then, up on the mountain, he'd pushed her too hard because of it. The kiss had put him off his mark.

It wouldn't happen again.

But if his friendship could help her find a new beginning...then maybe, just maybe...

While she sipped wine and sat with Lillie, Cole opened the door of the single cupboard in his outdoor kitchen, got out his marinade bag to start preparing the steaks. Having the woman there, petting his dog, made focus far more difficult than it should have been for such a simple task. The plastic vinegar bottle came first. Three short squirts. One. Two…

"I've never had a serious, long-term relationship."

The third squeeze blew the lid off the bottle, leaving him with a bag full of vinegar.

With Lindsay sitting on a wooden love seat glider, with Lillie's front paws in her lap. Lindsay's hands worked the dog's fur. Her face focused on the collie. But the words—*I've never had a serious, long-term relationship*—were for him.

A breakthrough moment.

Clearly a conscious decision. He dumped most of the vinegar, glad that she'd been looking at Lillie when he'd pulled his little trick. "Why is that?" he asked, keeping his tone casual. He was a friend, helping a new friend. Added Worcestershire sauce. Sealed the bag and shook.

"I never met anyone I wanted to spend that much time with."

After dropping two filets in the bag, he fumbled with the seal. A closure he could normally work with one hand and probably in his sleep. "You're only twenty-eight—you have lots of time."

"Did you know that thirty-five is considered a geriatric pregnancy? Though maybe that term isn't used as much anymore. With medical advances, most babies delivered to women in their later thirties are born perfectly normal…"

She sounded like a textbook. Her tendency toward verbosity had been evident a couple of other times during the past week. Generally, when she'd been discussing herself.

Cole didn't mean to notice, didn't consciously try, the observations just came to him. Always had.

"I take it that impromptu OB lesson stems from your desire to have kids someday?" He grinned at her. Tilted the newly sealed marinade bag back and forth enough to ensure full coverage for the steaks. Waiting for the answer.

He'd been teasing her.

If she didn't want kids, he had nothing more to worry about in terms of failing himself and jumping on a train bound to crash.

"I wanted two by the time I was thirty." She could have been discussing the salad he'd just pulled out to go with the steaks. He liked to add the dressing early, let the vegetables soak it up a bit.

And shouldn't be feeling quite as pleased by her response as he was.

"Why thirty?" he asked, keeping things casual.

"So that I'd be young enough to have more if I made it through the terrible twos."

He nodded. Tossed vegetables. While internally, he was loudly noting that the woman didn't have a significant other, and wanted kids.

Both of which fit him perfectly.

She wasn't there to fit him. Not for a while at any rate.

But if she ended up staying in Shelter Valley...

He returned the salad to the small outdoor refrigerator.

"I don't want my child to be without siblings."

Cole pulled up from the built-in door so fast he hit his head on the cupboard above the tiled counter. Not enough to hurt. It was only a graze at the edge. But the little knock was a warning to him. He'd pushed too hard on the mountain.

He needed to get himself in check. And then stay there.

A challenge he'd never had before, oddly enough. Even with Nicky. He'd been thrilled when she'd agreed to marry him. But he'd never lost his stride.

"You didn't like being an only child," he guessed then, grabbing his beer and joining Lindsay at the outdoor seating nook. Lillie looked over at him.

She always watched his movements. It was what she did.

But that look.

The kiss.

He glanced outward. "The view over the mountains is great at sunset."

Which wouldn't be happening for another hour or more.

Still…

No tension.

No tension. Each breath repeated the mandate.

No tension.

Not of the sexual kind.

Or emotional unrest brought on by him.

Hers, he could handle.

Settling back in the big wooden made-to-order chair with the cushioned pads the Wilson children had given him for Christmas one year, he watched the slender cord of Lindsay's neck as she glanced toward the mountains not too far in the distance. Saw her begin the soft, slow back and forth motion of the glider that could soothe her if she needed. Or let it.

"Did you like being an only child?" she asked him, and he took note. She'd had the opportunity to change the subject. Hadn't. Meant she was going somewhere with it.

"Not particularly," he told her. Then, in light of keeping the personal revelations mutual, he added, "But I'd say my size bothered me more than being an only kid. I was both tall and broad, and with the red curly hair…" He shrugged, then said, "By the time I was in high school, though, I'd grown into my skin. And a few other guys had caught up with me in height so it wasn't so bad."

If he gave her vulnerability, she'd be more comfortable giving it back if she wanted to. Or so he told himself. Truth was, he had no idea why he'd just said what he had. Who cared how big he was in second grade? They were adults. Decades past those years.

He sipped from his beer. Watched her hand lightly moving in the fur on Lillie's neck. Couldn't figure out why the woman was affecting him so strongly. And not just sexually. He'd long since learned to take it or leave it when it came to his female companions. Take what they wanted to offer, and leave everything else.

"I wasn't just an only child, I was an only grandchild."

Still not looking at him. He watched her. But stayed

silent. If she needed to pretend he wasn't there, silence was the most he could give her.

No hiding his big frame.

Almost as though she'd read his mind, she looked over at him. "I never knew my father."

Remaining still, he waited. She'd lied to him? He felt more curiosity, concern, than blame.

"My grandparents told me he was a…businessman. He ran out on my mom when she told him she was pregnant." She swallowed, but not from her glass. Just a notable throat movement. As though swallowing was difficult.

"After Mom had me, she went back to getting wasted, like she had for a time in high school."

Stay-at-home mom. Clearly that story hadn't been as charming as it had sounded the day before, either.

He got what she was doing. Making amends for her abrupt disappearance during their mountain picnic. And as much as he wanted to hear every word she chose to share, he didn't want her baring her soul to him as some kind of penance.

"Lindsay," he spoke softly, his glance completely serious. "You don't have to do this."

She frowned. "You want me to stop?" Then with a nod, "Too much, huh? I knew it was. I never talk about it. Never have. It's so…in the past and—"

"Hey," he cut her off. "It's not too much. Nothing about you is too much. Not here. Just ask Lillie." He was floundering. Turned to the better authority. Took a breath, then, leaning forward, with his hands clasped, said, "I want to hear what you're saying. Very much. I just don't want you to feel obligated…"

What in the hell was *wrong* with him?

Lillie stood, put her front paws in Lindsay's lap again. The artist smiled then, her hand on Lillie's back, and looked over at Cole. "My mom died of an accidental overdose when I was a baby."

"Did your grandparents try to contact your father?"

"No. What was the point? His actions had already proven him unfit. And the state had no means to find him. My birth certificate says father unknown."

"Did they ever disclose his identity to you?"

She looked him straight in the eye. "No."

"Your grandparents…are they still alive?"

"Yes. In San Diego. Still living in the house where I grew up."

And there he had it.

The heartache she'd been hiding.

All of the physical beauty in the world didn't cover up the truth she carried inside. Neither of her parents had found her worthy enough to be there for her.

"You know your parents' choices were no reflection on you." He said the words because they were glaringly there. Not because he expected them to help.

"I know," she said, still meeting his gaze as she sent him a kind smile. "Which is why I don't talk about any of it. I've built a good life, and that speaks for itself."

Yet…he saw something in her gaze…a longing maybe.

And had to look away before his need to provide swallowed him up.

## Chapter Ten

The steaks were cooked to perfection. And the conversation flowed as easily as the wine Cole poured. Feeling as though she'd climbed a much bigger mountain that evening than they had the day before, Lindsay let herself relax enough to just enjoy the night.

Something else she was realizing she didn't do in her real life. Why did there always have to be a purpose, a goal, for every waking moment?

"So, you want to help me pit the businesses in town against each other to raise money for Forever Friends?" she asked, as she and Cole lazed on his back porch watching the sun go down.

"I'm not sure I'd put it that way," he said with an easy grin. "But what do you have in mind?"

"Community spirit," she told him. "We can have a public leaderboard. Employees donate, or take donations, and we tally up donations every evening for a week or two. Maybe we have tiers...you know, top producer for companies with more than twenty employees, six to nineteen, and then five and under, or something. You'd know far better than I would how to divvy things up to make it a fair race. And you'd be the one to sell the project," she said, gaining momentum as she talked. Feeling the Warren-Smythe fire coming alive inside her. Welcoming it. "I'd handle all of the organizational aspects. The top-producing business gets kudos from the community. And say...a dinner in the park...free to everyone in town...thrown in honor of that business. We could even see about having an official community award presented to them. And if there's enough participation and interest, it could be set up to run every year, with the businesses voting on what cause they're going to donate to that year." She paused. "We could also charge a minimal fee for the town dinner, so that we have more money to donate..."

He was nodding, as though already on board.

She'd thought she'd have to sell him on the idea. Had another four ready to replace her first choice if he didn't think it would work.

"I'd want you to oversee all legalities, of course," she said then, rushing forward. She knew California charity laws. And still had a team of lawyers on staff of every charity for which she served as chief fundraising officer. But as Lindsay Warren, she couldn't use them. And with the charity being local, she most certainly didn't want to land someone in trouble with state tax ramifications.

Fifteen minutes passed as Cole talked about different ways to engage businesses, figuring he'd be able to get pretty much everyone in town in on the project. Talked about an end-of-the-summer community park event to award the winners. Even mentioned a local band he knew he could coax into performing. And suggested that maybe they open up the possibility of participating businesses being able to set up booths to sell their wares, or advertise their services.

When he started talking about rivalries and the lengths some had gone to over a holiday decorating contest one year, he had her laughing out loud.

She'd been planning events—most much larger with considerable dollar amounts and celebrities—for half a dozen years. Loved her work. And couldn't ever remember emitting a belly laugh during a planning session.

And, though it would be tempting, she couldn't blame her joie de vivre solely on the wine she'd consumed. She'd shared bottles of wine during some late-night sessions in the past. More than she'd had that night.

Maybe she could blame a little bit of the fire in her nether regions on the liquid consumption. Statistics did point to the fact that alcohol increased libido. But it had never affected her that way in the past.

"We make a good team," she said as she finished off the list she'd been making on her phone while they spoke. She'd get a proposal typed up before bed that night. Cole had already offered to be present during her upcoming meeting with Mariah Montford. Had even taken a moment while she'd been thumb typing notes to call the horse therapist and set up a lunch appointment with her at Elite the following day.

Cole's silence rang loudly in the space that had been filled with constant conversation and energetic exchange over the past several minutes.

And she heard her words. *We make a good team.*

At home, Lindsay always ended her work sessions with a positive note to those working with her. She truly appreciated the efforts everyone put forth to help those less fortunate and strove to make certain that everyone she dealt with felt valued.

But a good team—when it was only her and Cole?

She looked up at him, standing next to her at the railing on his back deck. He'd been reading over her list, to make certain she hadn't forgotten anything. She should have just handed him her phone.

He was going to kiss her again. She felt it coming. Waited for his lips to descend. While a part of her recognized that Lillie was still sleeping on the padded couch next to Cole's chair.

As though she wasn't bothered at all about the improprieties that were about to happen.

More likely, the old girl was exhausted at the end of a long day and needed her sleep.

Crazy to think that Lillie wasn't jumping down to shove herself between them because the dog approved of their closeness and what it might bring.

Cole's lips weren't lowering. His gaze locked with hers. He was there. Into her. But not moving.

She had to go. Needed to say so.

"The end of the summer, the celebration in the park,

that could be my last weekend in town," she said pain-
fully. Her short-term apartment lease was up then. Her
Christmas card designs would be finished before that.
And while she had little doubt that Elite would assign
other design work to her, she just couldn't see a way
for Lindsay Warren-Smythe to have any future in Shelter Valley.

"My grandparents want me home," she said then,
finding the explanation so naturally, she knew it was
right. "They're all the family I've got."

And there was no way Cole would leave Shelter Valley.

Nor could he, for her. Because in San Diego, she
was Lindsay Warren-Smythe. And if Brent Wilson ever
heard that name…

He was still looking down at her, his green eyes darkened in the dusk that had fallen. Hadn't moved enough
to allow even another inch of space in between them.

"I want you to kiss me," she whispered then. "I just
don't want you to get hurt."

"I've had other short-term relationships."

"You have?"

He nodded. Didn't elaborate on when or with who.

"You go in knowing it's only for the moment," he
said then and she wanted so badly to believe him. "But
I don't want to hurt you, either."

She didn't get hurt. Not romantically. She'd have to
be able to fall in love to do that and so far, she hadn't
given herself any hope that she had that ability.

Desire took over his expression, building in his slum-
berous gaze, shining from his slightly parted lips.

If she stepped away, she'd be rejecting him, right? She couldn't reject him.

As badly as she wanted him, it would be a lie to reject him. Send him a false message.

"I suggest we take this up at a later date," Cole said just as she started to lift herself up to his lips. "We both have to work early in the morning and you need to prepare for our meeting with Mariah. I should take you home." He hadn't moved.

But his gaze had softened enough that she took a deep breath.

Nodded.

And as disappointment washed through her in waves, she was also relieved.

Cole had learned early how to make temporary friends. How to enjoy people, get close to them quickly, knowing that he only had a window of time with them. That either he, or they, would come home from school one day to a parent's news that they were being transferred, and off they'd go to another new world. You shed a few tears—when you were young enough that you didn't know better—and then you found new friends to have fun with.

Shelter Valley had changed all of that for him.

Because he'd also learned young that he didn't want to spend his life in temporary relationships. He wanted lifelong friends. Stability for himself and any family he created.

That next week, the two worlds seemed to meld for him. The security of a solid home in a town he loved allowed him to get closer to a woman even knowing that his time with her would be short. Mia Jones, owner of Homestead Ranch, but also an accidental social media influencer, had come to the lunch on Tuesday with Mariah, wanting to do all she could to help with Lindsay's fundraising venture. Mia ended up taking over publicity for them. Mariah provided all official content regarding the work that Forever Friends did, including, at Lindsay's encouragement, real-life stories of people who'd been helped by the horse rescue program.

Some would remain anonymous, but as their small team reached out, they found many former Forever Friends clients who wanted to help spread the word.

Cole got almost one hundred percent local business participation, in four different categories. And Mia grew the project to a wider area, setting up online donations where businesses from outside Shelter Valley could join any of the four established categories and be entered to win a shout-out on Mia's social media accounts.

No matter how the project grew, Lindsay was right there, on top of things, organizing it all, making spreadsheets, keeping track, monitoring. All in her spare time.

Project Forever Friends, as their efforts had been named, had Cole and Lindsay together every evening over the next week, as they finalized plans and got things in place for an official rollout the following Monday at the open of business in Shelter Valley. But they were rarely alone.

More his call than was absolutely necessary.

He wanted to give Lindsay time to get to know the real him. The working, Shelter Valley citizen guy who lived a relatively simple life. And if she still thought she was attracted to him once things rolled out and their nightly work quieted down some, then, maybe, he'd kiss her again.

And see where it led.

Or, maybe not. The decision didn't have to be made ahead of time. Or at all, if that's how things fell.

Saturday afternoon, though, when he and Lindsay ended up alone on the floor of her apartment—affixing labels she'd designed and had printed to the collection jars she'd ordered, in preparation for their delivery to all of the participating Shelter Valley businesses the next day—he had little doubt as to how things were falling for the gorgeous blonde.

Barefoot, and in a flowing spaghetti-strap sundress, she kept bumping his bare feet with the tips of her toes. Maybe because the space was entirely too small for the project at hand. He was pretty sure not. Lindsay was deliberately teasing him.

Lillie, stretched out on the sheet Lindsay had laid on the apartment's couch for her, seemed to notice the contact, but didn't mind all that much.

By the fifth toe touch, Cole was done waiting for time to pass. "You better be sure about the force you're letting loose there," he said aloud with a half-choking chuckle, nodding toward where all five of her painted left toenails were resting against the side and top of his foot.

"Oh, so you do still feel a little something for me," she said back with complete sass. But the grin on her face wasn't casual at all. Her lips trembled. And her eyes burned with promise.

"Lindsay…"

"Yes, Cole?" She ran a tongue over her lips.

"You just put that label on upside down."

Her fingers shook as she peeled. Her toes left his skin as she stood to get some glass cleaner and a cloth to take the sticky glue residue off the jar.

And Cole cursed himself for defusing the moment. He wanted her so badly he ached nights. Took multiple cold showers a day.

He could handle her eventual leaving.

But wasn't going to put himself through another time of finding out that the woman in his arms really wasn't as into him as she'd thought she was. He had to know that she saw him as he really was before he let himself have what he suspected was going to be the best sex of his life.

Past and future.

No one was going to be as fantastic as Lindsay Warren.

His head knew it. His gut knew it. And his perpetual hardness around her—was pretty much done along with the rest of him. Done waiting.

And how did he know for sure that Lindsay was really into him? As a woman was into a man that she didn't just want as a friend?

Where was the evidence? The proof?

When had he become such a flaming idiot on the matter? Who cared who liked who more if the sex was mutually great and no one got hurt when she left?

There'd be regret, sure, when he watched her drive out of town. If, indeed, she ended up going. She hadn't mentioned it, but there was always a chance her grandparents could fall in with Shelter Valley. Be agreeable to moving there.

And if she left town and he'd passed on the opportunity to know her as closely as he possibly could?

Top-of-the-line disappointment there.

By the time the jars were done, in boxes ready to be loaded into his SUV for their deliveries the next day, Cole had pretty much used up every thought he had on the matter of sex with Lindsay Warren.

And was getting ready to carry out the first batch of boxes when Lindsay called out to him. "Cole?"

"Yeah?"

"I have no idea how to come on to a guy, and I think I'm doing it all wrong." The words were bold and she was looking him right in the eye.

His loose-fitting cotton shorts were suddenly tight beneath the oversize short-sleeved shirt he'd pulled on that morning.

"You've never come on to a guy." Disbelieving statement more than question.

And when she shook her head, he said, "I find that hard to believe."

"I've never wanted one enough to bother," she said then.

More like, she'd never had to bother, he figured. As beautiful as she was, any guy she wanted would be hitting on her, first.

With him being the exception.

Because he was behaving like a very not-smart man.

"Not even ones with whom I've been in relationships. Which, come to think of it, is probably why they were all so brief."

So was that her attraction to him? The fact that he was holding out when she'd been able to have any man she wanted?

He'd gotten over Nicky. Over his other failures to raise more than friendship in a woman's heart. But if he started something with Lindsay and she decided she just wanted to be friends?

*Good God, man. You're thirty-one years old. Not fifteen.*

"You make me wet, just looking at you," she said then. Without the least bit of a sexy tone in her voice. "Just stating the facts, man, just stating the facts," was what her words sounded like to him. "I dream about your lips on mine again, and then moving all over me. I want to sit on top of you. To feel you over me. And, oh lord, in me. All the way in. Again and again. I want to rub my hands over that massive chest of yours and to kiss your sweet stomach. You're driving me over the edge here, Cole, and as long as you're as good with short-term relationships as you say you are, the only conclusion I can come to is that you aren't as attracted to me as I am to you."

*He* was getting moist at his tip. Knew what that meant.

"Anyway, I just needed to get it said. Get it out there. Acknowledge the situation and move on from it…you know, the whole elephant on the table th—"

His lips cut off the rest of whatever she'd been going to say.

There'd been enough words. Enough thinking.

It was time to pleasure the most incredible woman he'd ever known.

No questions asked. And no looking back.

Every look in his eye, every touch of his fingers, his body, every sound he made, the woodsy freshly-showered scent of him, the softness of his belly as she sat upon it, all of it consumed Lindsay, drove her, became a part of her.

Her body needed, demanded, every ounce of her. For once in her lifetime, her mind was completely silent.

Cole played her as though she were a priceless instrument, strumming lightly here, more powerfully there. Her hands, her lips, couldn't get enough of him. The dance went on and on. No judgment, no thought, no ideas, even, just riding waves that were the whole world.

When he finally entered her, holding himself on his elbows so his size was a gentle touch rather than crushing, she cried out. Again and again. Out of her mind with sensation that spiraled through her entire body. Bucking up to him, she rode him fast, slowly, and fast again.

Until, like winning choreography, they came together, seconds and seconds of unbelievable pleasure.

Once wasn't enough. She knew it as soon as her breathing started to slow. He'd pulled out of her but was growing again.

Twice wasn't enough, either.

She laughed at his readiness. He quickly showed her her own. And grinned at her shock.

When passion finally had to take a break, to give their bodies time to replenish, Lindsay remained in the aftermath of euphoria. A soft and quiet place that held her with tenderness.

Just as Cole did. Both arms resting loosely on her as she lay sprawled over him.

His muscles were magnificent. Huge and hard and yet offering promise of care and protection. A sense that there'd be no job too big for him to accomplish. No strength more powerful than his own.

At some point after he pulled her sheet up over them, she felt a slight depression on the end of the bed.

Lillie had joined them.

As she fell asleep, Lindsay accepted the old girl's blessing.

## *Chapter Eleven*

Cole got Lillie's message. Fun was over, time to go home. The old girl had been patient, waiting out on the couch. Still, he put her off another half hour as he lay there in Lindsay's rented bed and held her close while she slept.

He was making a memory.

One that would bring him pleasure for the rest of his life.

Cole Bennet, the guy who was more often the friend than the lover, had driven a beautiful woman to the point of complete, mindless explosion.

He was smiling as he gently rolled over, untangled himself, kissed her and grabbed his clothes to dress out in the hallway. Smiled all the way home, too.

Grinned the next night, too, when he left her bed.

And for much of the next week as he and Lindsay

delivered their jars. She collected them every night—
and he smiled some more as he heard stories she'd been
told from the various citizens she was getting to know.
Every business tallied their day's collection, and then
Lindsay did a recount at night before depositing the
money in an account she'd opened specifically for the
Project Forever Friends funds.

As great an artist as she was, Lindsay was showing
him a side of herself that was equally impressive. Her
business mind easily was on par with his.

Which made him wonder why her art wasn't support-
ing her any better than a tiny apartment, an ancient car
and scant wardrobe. Not only was he seeing her in the
same five or six outfits, he'd gotten a glimpse of her
closet when he'd been leaving her bedroom that first
night. There were six hangers. Period.

Granted, she wasn't sure she was staying. Had probably left things in storage. But that car of hers would
have held a lot more than she'd brought with her.

As though she'd never planned on staying?

Because he had other obligations several nights that
next week he was only able to have sex with Lindsay
once more after Sunday's repeat, at her apartment again
on Wednesday night after a council meeting. And with
Lillie waiting at home for him. The experience was
quick, but as mind-blowing the third night as it had
been the first. It was as though every fantasy he'd ever
had, every dream he'd dared to dream when he'd been
younger, had come true in her.

Yeah, if she left, he'd miss the hell out of her. But
he'd still be glad that he'd known her.

Was one hundred percent certain he'd made the right choice to be with her.

And at work…her art was glorious, the bright colors and muted tones mingling much like the holiday did. Glitz, excitement and gifts, and stable with a manger filled with hay and a newborn baby. While she didn't depict the two sets of images together, she managed to get the feeling of awe, humility and miraculous joy into every design.

She didn't report to him. Chief of personnel had no meat in the company's product. But after he saw her initial designs, he made certain that Brent Wilson knew to get a look at them as well.

He needn't have bothered, he discovered as, still sitting in his boss and mentor's office Friday morning, Wilson showed him the concept board the art director had delivered just that day.

"Look at Lindsay Warren's output," Brent told Cole. "Her designs are magnificent. Easily our best work. What's your take on her settling in here? Any complaints about her or from her?"

"None."

"You're working with her on Project Friends Forever. You get a sense that she's enjoying Shelter Valley? Making friends?"

"Ah, Brent, that line of questioning creates an issue for me."

Cole saw the older man's brows draw together and was surprised at his own lawyerly tone. He owed Brent so much, admired the man more than any other, and so he had to be honest with him.

"Lindsay has given me some confidences," he said slowly. "I'm not at liberty to share them."

When he saw Brent's brows change from frowning to raised with interest, he groaned inwardly. The conversation was unexpected. He hadn't been prepared.

"You're seeing her personally?" Brent asked, not quite smiling, but clearly showing pleasure at the idea.

"Yes, but nothing long-term," he quickly stated the important facts. "And as to the rest, I can tell you that she has grandparents in San Diego who miss her."

The older man's gaze sharpened. He pinned Cole with it for longer than was comfortable. And then, his expression softening again, he said, "I guess it's up to you to convince her that we'll miss her more if she decides not to stay." Brent nodded then, as if coming to a decision. "Offer her more money. Enough that she won't be able to refuse," he said, naming an amount. "She'll make it back for us in a year."

Money had never been an issue for Brent, but that was going far, even for him.

On the other hand, Lindsay's work was superior to anything else they'd seen.

And… Cole wanted her to stay as badly as Brent did.

Probably worse.

Obviously worse.

Not that he was going to share that tidbit with his boss, no matter how long they'd been family to each other.

He couldn't let himself hope that a substantial raise would sway Lindsay's ability to stay in Shelter Valley.

But was eager to make the offer, just in case. He'd do about anything to sweeten that deal.

"Emily and I are having movie night tonight with the kids," Brent said then. "Emily's making her kettle corn. Genre's comedy. Kyle's turn to pick the films. See if you can get Lindsay to join us…"

It was more of an order than request. Not at all the norm between him and Brent. But then, Cole hadn't told his friend that he was seeing someone since Nicky.

A decade ago.

"I'll issue the invitation, but I can't guarantee she'll come," he said, standing. Made it to the door, then turned. "But if she does… I swear to God, Brent, if you or Emily or the kids make it more than it is, I'll get up and walk out." He'd never been more serious about anything in his life.

Brent's grin didn't bring out the responding senti-ment in him. Seeing Cole's unrelenting expression, the older man sobered immediately, and said, "I'll talk to them and you have my word, we'll respect your feel-ings, Cole."

He nodded.

And walked out.

Leaving work early on Friday, Lindsay made her money collections and headed home, eager to add to the impressive balance that had grown in the project's bank. In just one week's time, they'd managed to raise almost as much as she'd collect at a black-tie affair buzz-ing with California's most wealthy donors.

She wanted the work done because Cole had invited

her to have dinner with him at his place. He'd come get her. They still weren't going public with their personal friendship, though the project had made it easier for them to be seen in town together.

As busy as they'd both been, she hadn't had a chance to see Lillie since the old girl had jumped off her bed for a second time Sunday night, except for a brief moment on Wednesday, and she was looking forward to some minutes soaking up the collie's wisdom, too.

And...she wasn't going to kid herself; she wanted to have sex with Cole in his bed. It was bigger. His feet wouldn't hang off the end. And it was his. Would smell of him.

Plus, she wouldn't be left lying alone naked when they were through. She'd be getting up and getting dressed along with him, for him to drive her home.

As much as she might like to fantasize about staying the night, she knew she wouldn't. That she couldn't. There had to be boundaries lest they both forget, for a time, that they weren't building toward something more.

Though, in some of her quietest moments, she wondered if there was any way for her to stay in Shelter Valley. Or at least visit often.

There wasn't. She knew that. While she'd managed to steer personally clear of Brent Wilson during her weeks in town, she'd fully gleaned the picture of the man she'd come to find. Anytime anyone heard that she worked at Elite, she heard another story about something good the man had done for whoever she was talking to or someone they knew closely. She'd talked to Savannah twice during the past five days and so far, Sierra's Web had found nothing negative about the man. No police record. Not even a driving violation. He paid his taxes. Had A-plus credit.

Every day that passed, every story she heard, the complete lack of sins in the man's history—all solidified her knowledge that she had to leave Shelter Valley— and him and his family—undisturbed. She couldn't hurt any of them with the truth.

Brent Wilson had done something horrible in his youth. But he'd apparently spent the rest of his life making good. Had it just been between him and her, she still might have considered telling him who she was. He was twenty-eight years too late, but a part of her wanted to be his daughter.

But there was no way she'd hurt his wife, or his kids, with his shameful past. Or risk betraying their trust in him. She'd grown up without him, but that shouldn't mean that Kyle and Kaitlin and Kerby had to. They weren't at fault for what had happened years before they were born.

Nor was Emily.

Which meant that she had to slide quietly away.

She was the one who'd started the quest. It was up to her to end it.

As soon as the project's award ceremony was complete.

Until then, she wanted to soak up every ounce of Shelter Valley air that she could. Save it in a hand-blown glass bottle on a chain and wear it around her neck forever.

And savor every second with the one man who'd

found a way to unlock the sensual woman locked inside her. She'd miss Cole like crazy.

Didn't even want to think about leaving him behind. But knew she couldn't ask him to come with her, either. She couldn't tell him the truth about herself. He was family to Brent as much as anyone.

In her down moments she contemplated the idea of Ms. Bohemian being forever email buddies with Cole, like she was with her seventy-year-old Canadian friend she'd met at a show. But knew, realistically, even that would never work. She and Cole were sexually attracted. San Diego was only a six-hour drive away.

He could always show up at a Lindsay Warren show, though. Her appearances were always on her website. They could have clandestine weekends together...

Her phone ringing interrupted Lindsay's train of thought to bring her back to the pile of money still sitting unsorted on the table in her tiny, temporary apartment.

Phone first. Cole.

"Change of plans for tonight, if you're up for it," he said as soon as she picked up.

"We go straight to bed and have a midnight snack for dinner?"

His deep, appreciative chuckle made her shiver in the most delicious way.

"Can I tempt you with comedy, kettle corn and then bed?"

"You want kettle corn for dinner?" Granted, skipping meals wasn't a good plan. The man had to eat.

"We've been invited to the Wilsons' for movie night."

The words were a death knell to her enthusiasm. Replacing anticipation with dread.

Was it too late to claim illness? A sudden headache?

Or would spending an evening with her father and his family send her home with a sense of that warmth? Filling her future with something besides hate and resentment for the man?

*It could also somehow give us an insight into the man's faults*, Warren-Smythe reminded her. A man's home was the first place to look.

She'd come to town to find her father.

How could she turn down the chance to observe him as a family man?

"Brent and Emily had a home theater built onto their home when Kyle was little," Cole was saying, as though trying to convince her that the invitation wasn't horrible news. "They've held regular movie nights with the kids ever since, trading off between genres and who gets to pick the films. Tonight's Kyle's turn. He's the fifteen-year-old." His tone, his delivery, didn't carry pressure. Just information to use in the arriving at whatever decision she chose to make.

Because he didn't pressure. He gave insight, and support, and respected others' rights to make their own choices. Like Nicky. She'd left him at the altar and the man was going to be godfather to her firstborn son.

Sex aside, Cole Bennet was the most compelling man she'd ever known.

"Do you want me to get out of it?" he asked when her silence hung on the line.

She dreaded going. And she wanted to go. To meet

her half siblings. "What's tonight's genre?" She bought herself more time.

"Comedy."

A fifteen-year-old's idea of comedy might not be hers.

"We could come back here afterward," Cole said then. "We'd be home no later than ten."

Clearly, he was familiar with movie night. Maybe a regular for it, too?

"And still have time before that midnight snack." His tone reminding her of their naked bodies on her hard little mattress, his mouth against her ear, telling her what he was going to do to her next.

His message—they were still going to have sex. Either way.

"Well, as long as I still get that snack, then I'm in," she said, feeling slightly excited, and kind of sick to her stomach, too. "How about if I order a pizza and we can stop at the mountain overlook to eat it on the way over?"

They'd never shared any of the dinner pie, but had discovered that they both favored thin crust with ham and onion during a conversation with the owner of the Italian eatery in town.

"Better get a single-serving container of plain hamburger for Lillie. She'll smell the pizza and be expecting it."

Lindsay's laugh bubbled up out of her. And she was still smiling as she hung up and dialed the phone to order dinner.

He'd way overreacted with Brent. The second Cole entered the other man's house, ushering in an absolutely gorgeous Lindsay in her white-and-red tie-dyed spaghetti-strap dress with the red jeweled flip-flops, he was on display.

Not because his own beige shorts and light brown shirt were anything different than he normally wore, but because he'd drawn attention to the fact that Lindsay was important to him. He'd actually given Brent an ultimatum. Something he'd never done before in his life.

And the entire family had clearly been put on alert.

The kids all greeted Lindsay with friendly smiles and questions about her art—Kaitlin taking her to her room for a second to show her the drawings she was working on—but they didn't joke or fool around with Brent at all.

Not that Lindsay would know any differently, but as the movie started, a classic slapstick involving kids in a school hijacking a snowplow, he could hardly stand how little Brent laughed. The man had taken a seat with Emily in the row behind he and Lindsay, with the three kids in the front row, as always, and the fourth, last row of theater seating left for Lillie. Anytime Cole turned his head, his peripheral vision showed Brent watching him and Lindsay, not the movie.

Granted, they'd seen the film half a dozen times since Kyle had started on his old iconic movie enthusiasm several years before, but Brent always laughed his way through it.

That night the kids made up for their father, laughing so hard that he caught Lindsay smiling at them instead of the movie.

But overall, as soon as the closing credits started to

roll and the lights came back up, he was out of there. Good-nights were short and sweet, made so by Kaitlin begging her parents to let them watch one more, since it wasn't a school night, and Brent complying.

And then he forgot all about movies and family nights as Lillie led the way into the house, and he and Lindsay undressed, stumbling together to get to his bed, the second they'd followed the dog in from his garage.

He gave Lindsay all of his attention, his thoughts, let himself go completely, while they made love with each other.

Twice.

And stopped for fast-food ice-cream cones on the way back to her place, laughing about their mutual appetites, while Lillie sat in the backseat chomping one of the treats he kept for her in his glove box.

He saw Lindsay to her door. Slipped inside to give her a long, hungry kiss good-night, and then listened for her to lock up behind him before rejoining Lillie for the ride home.

The girl was already in the front seat when he climbed into the SUV.

Was watching him with question in her solemn gaze.

"I have it under control, girl," he assured her.

But he wasn't sure he did.

And had a feeling she doubted him, too.

## Chapter Twelve

Lindsay lost herself in Cole Friday night. She'd eaten ice cream and laughed. But the second she locked the door behind him, she started to sob. Big, gulping, gut-wrenching sobs.

She wasn't a crier. Didn't let herself want any one thing enough to make it worth crying over. But without her consent, twenty-eight years of anguish broke out of her and just kept coming. She quieted down for a bit. Made herself some chamomile tea. Tried to watch some lighthearted videos on her phone.

Until the tears trickled out to block her view and the storm came again. Raging over and over throughout the night.

She'd looked at Kaitlin's drawings—her little sister who was talented just like she was—had seen the room dotted with posters and notes and a bulletin board filled with greeting cards from birthdays and Valentine's, Christmas and even a Thanksgiving one. Of course, with her father owning a card-making company, the board made sense.

Lindsay would have loved to have had one.

As she wiped away slowing tears around three in the morning, she knew she didn't begrudge Kaitlin or Kyle or little Kerby any of their father's love, or their home or security. She'd had all three, too. And wanted it for the three of them.

Needed it for them now that she'd actually met them. Had looked in the eyes of her siblings and felt a connection that was valid and deep.

She'd learned two things that night about love. It could exist without time and shared memories. It didn't have to be returned to be real.

She cried for her mother. For her own losses.

And she cried knowing that she was going to have to leave them all and never come back.

Mostly she just released a couple of decades of grief, and woke late Sunday morning with a stronger heart.

And a promise to herself that she'd squeeze every single bit of joy and memory she could out of her remaining weeks in Shelter Valley. And store them in conscious thought, keeping them close and accessible for the rest of her life.

She also decided that once she returned to San Diego, she was getting a dog. Maybe two of them. So they wouldn't be lonely during Lindsay's long days at work.

And when she got to be Lindsay Warren—she'd take them with her everywhere she went, like Cole did Lillie. To the shows. To the beach. They'd have their orders at her favorite restaurants. And share the front seat of her SUV with her.

Over the next weeks, she'd watch Brent Wilson from afar. Learn his mannerisms and his smiles. There was no point in furthering the relationship. The dead end had to remain what it was. But she could take a sense of him—because a part of her was him—with her into the future.

And Cole...

Well, he was always going to be top billing for her.

On Monday at work, he offered her a magnanimous raise to sign a year's contract, by Lindsay Warren standards, but hadn't shown any surprise or undue disappointment when she'd turned it down. Because that was Cole. His attractiveness wasn't just skin-deep.

Maybe the future held someone else she could love and marry, with whom she'd someday have children, but there'd never be another Cole Bennet. He'd shown her who she was as a woman.

Had brought Ms. Bohemian and Warren-Smythe face-to-face, eye to eye and heart to heart. In just a few short weeks, he'd taken her permanently separated pieces and had shown her how they fit.

His glue would always be holding her together.

She had it all figured out, as was the Warren-Smythe way, right up until the following Wednesday when Savannah called. She'd had a fast dinner with Cole, followed by a slightly longer quickie in the bedroom, before he'd had to leave for a Rotary Club meeting. Was really proud of how both of them were sucking up every ounce of air from the life they'd been given together, while fully accepting that it was going to end, as she picked up her friend's call.

"Okay, we found something."

Shaking her head, still lost in the aftereffects of Cole's lovemaking, she said, "What?" Trying to figure out what Savannah was talking about.

"The team went back further, looked at Brent's family growing up," Savannah was saying, and Lindsay finally realized what was going on.

"It's okay," she said then. She didn't need to know about the man's childhood. It had no bearing on her future. "I'm done," she told Savannah. "The quest is over."

"You're leaving Shelter Valley? Today? You need a place to stay tonight?"

"No." She shook her head, wondering how much to tell her friend. And how much was sacred between her and Cole. "I'm going to stay until I've finished the Forever Friends project. I just don't need anything more on Brent Wilson. Whatever he was in the past, he's a decent man now. Has a lot of people who love and depend on him. I'm not going to interfere with that." For what? Her own vindication?

She wasn't a vindictive person.

"No good would come of it," she said then.

"Okay." Savannah wasn't arguing, but she didn't sound as though she approved of Lindsay's choice, either. Or thought it was the best one.

Lindsay slowed down. Let her brain take over, as she always had when it came to matters of her deepest heart.

"You found something I'm going to want to know about, didn't you?"

"I'd want to know if it was me."

"You know me, though. I've found my peace and that's all I was after." But what had Savannah found? Did it explain why her father had left? Could she have that final part of the puzzle to put her own past to rest? Was that what Savannah was trying to tell her?

"I do know you," was all Savannah said, but it was enough.

"Tell me."

"His dad died in prison a few years back. He'd been serving life for a series of armed robberies with aggravators."

She swallowed. One grandfather a well-respected, wealthy philanthropist. The other a criminal who died behind bars? She hadn't needed to know that.

"His mom worked a couple of jobs to support him and his older brother."

"He has a brother?"

She had an uncle?

"Yes, but from what we can tell they haven't been in touch for more than two decades. The last known communication we could find, via a social media site, was one blocking the other."

"Who blocked who?"

"The older brother blocked him."

Lindsay didn't know what to make of that. And still didn't know why Savannah thought the information pertinent to her.

"The older brother—his name is James, by the way—

has a pretty long record, Lins. Has been in and out of jail for the past twenty years. All on drug charges. Selling them, mostly. To well-to-do kids."

Sick to her stomach, gut sinking so low she had to sit down, Lindsay said, "You're about to tell me that my father was my mother's dealer." She preempted the blow.

"Either that, or his brother was," Savannah said. "Brent was arrested once, along with his brother, but was never charged with anything, which was why we never found a criminal record for him. But after finding his brother's criminal record, the team looked at the arrest records..."

There was more...some details that didn't really register...condolences from her friend, but Lindsay was outside it all.

Taking in what she'd learned, for hours after the call ended. Absorbing the information into her soul for future keeping.

Whether the drugs had come from James or Brent, her mother had trusted the man who'd given her the drugs that had killed her. Taking them had been her choice. Lindsay knew that.

But if Brent had hung around, if he'd cared enough to try to help, rather than making money off a girl who cared about him—a life might have been saved. Lindsay might have grown up with a parent.

Assuming Brent knew.

Her brain blurted one thought after the other. He had to have known. He'd been arrested with his drug-dealing brother. He had to have known the charges.

And found a way out of them for himself.

Another long sleepless night followed Savannah's call, but Lindsay showed up at work on Thursday with strength and a new plan.

A new quest.

She was hanging around long enough to make certain that her three siblings were not being raised by a man who could still be quietly providing illegal substances to rich kids who could afford them.

His company, his great reputation, his wealth all colluded to make him the obvious cover. She just had to read the news to know that a lot of wealthy, well-respected and revered people had secrets. Some of them really bad ones.

Everyone had skeletons in their closets. No one was perfect.

She'd called Savannah back on her way to work. Had the entire Sierra's Web team looking at Elite Paper and Brent Wilson, anything and everything they could find, by any legal means, no matter the cost. She wanted to know if anyone associated with the man had had drug convictions. Or had any associations with rehab centers.

If there were any ties to Brent Wilson and any known cartel members.

And Cole?

He was her bright spot. The blessing in her possibly being in town longer.

She couldn't think about what would happen to him if he found out his mentor was using his life in Shelter Valley to deal illegal drugs behind the scenes.

Couldn't think about what it would do to Kaitlin and Kerby and Kyle, or to Emily. Or all of the people she worked with at Elite Paper. The dozens of folks she'd gotten to know during Project Forever Friends.

But neither could she walk away, suspecting, and doing nothing.

For the rest of that day, she lost herself in her art. Playing around with some all-occasion "thinking of you" designs. And when she shared an elevator down to the lobby with Brent Wilson and a group of upper management after work, when her father smiled at her. She smiled back.

And knew that, in her deepest heart, lingering inside Ms. Bohemian's soul, she wasn't looking for dirt on the man. She needed to clear his name.

Maybe for herself. Most definitely for the others.

Because if Sierra's Web could find out about his past, so could any other number of people who'd want to do him harm. He deserved a heads-up on that.

Not from her. But if need be, she could arrange something.

He'd left her and her mother at their most weak and vulnerable.

She might be her father's daughter, but she wasn't leaving him the way he'd left them.

When Brent Wilson called Cole into his office Friday morning, Cole entered with a bit of trepidation. Concerned about what he'd possibly shown the man regarding his personal relationship with their newest artist acquisition—in light of her recent refusal of their lucrative offer to her in exchange for the signing of a one-year contract.

Loath to offend the man who was most definitely family to him, he also wasn't a kid who needed, or in any way wanted, help, or any kind of advice, in the love department.

He was a grown man, eyes wide open, living life to the fullest.

Turned out, Brent just wanted to discuss a potential employee situation—a supervisor at the plant in Phoenix who'd been seen by a longtime friend of Brent's leaving an upscale restaurant the night before while heavily inebriated. According to the friend, the man had climbed into a car on his own, and driven away. Wanting to avoid any possible accidents, and save potentially lost lives, the friend had called the police, but the man's car had been parked in his driveway when the police caught up to it and no one had answered a knock at the door.

Disturbed by the account, Cole assured his boss that he'd set up a meeting with the man that afternoon and was on his way to the door when Brent stopped him with, "I had a meeting with Jeremy Weldon this morning." Elite's art director. Cole turned, dreading the worst. Lindsay had quit. Left without saying goodbye.

The thought lasted less than a second. She wouldn't go without finishing Project Forever Friends.

Or telling him.

"We'd like to do a Lindsay Warren Valentine's line, and need you to approach her with the offer."

Cole's defenses shot up. If Brent was trying to buy him more time to...

Time to what?

And…her own valentine line.

Genius.

Getting her to stay little bits at a time.

Who cared why Brent had made the offer?

With a nod, he agreed to approach Lindsay Warren with the opportunity. And left the room before he made more of a fool of himself in front of the man whose respect meant more to him than a few nights of great sex.

He'd blown it the week before over the movie night invitation. And had felt Brent's gaze on him all week—whether the sensation had been real, or born of his own inner conflict, he couldn't be sure.

If he didn't know better, he'd figure Lillie for carrying tales on him.

And for what?

Seizing the moment?

Entertaining the thoughts on the walk from Brent's office to his own, Cole shut his door with a bit more force than necessary, and no humor whatsoever.

He wasn't falling for Lindsay Warren.

Did he wish things were different and she could stay in Shelter Valley?

Hell, yes.

Would he follow her to San Diego if she asked?

No. Unequivocally. He was not giving up the life he'd built, the home he loved, on the off chance that a relationship with a woman he'd just met might work out.

No matter how compelling she was.

And that was all the answer anyone needed to fully grasp that he had things firmly under control where the gorgeous blonde was concerned.

Lindsay had been completely honest with him from the beginning. She was only offering a short-term partnering. And that offer had allowed him to fully engage with her in it.

He wouldn't have trusted anything more.

And was done thinking about it all.

## *Chapter Thirteen*

Lindsay didn't know what to think when Cole texted and asked her to come to his office late Friday afternoon. She'd been hired, originally, to work on a stream of all-occasion card designs and for the remainder of her tenure at Elite Paper she was giving them her best effort in that regard.

She'd turned down the lovely offer to sign a year's contract. In spite of the fact that it would have been Lindsay Warren's dream come true.

Or part of it, anyway.

Cole being the other part.

There really was no reason for the chief of personnel to have any further business with her.

Unless he wanted a quickie in his office.

He had a dinner party for the local elite to attend that night and would be out late. And after she collected and deposited the day's Forever Friends funds, she was driving into Phoenix to dine with Savannah—not that he knew that part. Or could know that Lindsay Warren-Smythe needed time in her own world to stay emotionally and mentally above water.

Still, she'd been thinking all day about his naked body touching hers.

If he'd been needing her as desperately...

His office door locked.

He had a couch.

And a desk.

Walking the breezeway in her silk-and-denim skirt, she got all hot and bothered just thinking about doing it on a desk.

Cole's desk.

What in the hell the man had done to her...

Or, she'd done to herself by setting Lindsay Warren free...

Still, she was wet and filled with anticipation when she approached Cole's closed door. And then stopped, taking a deep breath before entering.

And got a good look at herself.

Thinking only about her. What she needed and wanted.

And that was most definitely not why she was in Shelter Valley.

Feeling as though she'd been doused with a bucket of ice water, she knocked, waiting for Cole's "Enter" before turning the knob.

No more busting in on him as though she had the

right to the kind of emotions with him that prompted such action.

For a second, as their gazes met, the heat was back. Flooding her. Because his gaze was pretty clear as he eyed her up and down, practically stripping her.

And realized that maybe she misread the look, seeing a signal where there wasn't one, as, in a completely professional tone, he asked her to take a seat.

And then said, "I have an offer for you, but before I deliver it, I need you to know that I had absolutely nothing to do with it. Didn't even know about it until this morning."

Confused, wary, she nodded. "Okay." The word was almost an afterthought.

How could she know anything was okay when she had no idea what they were talking about? Or why Cole was acting so strange about whatever it was?

"Elite Paper would like to offer you your own Lindsay Warren Valentine line."

From the depths of confusion and concern, to elation in a split second, Lindsay sat perfectly still. Holding her hands tightly clasped together.

"The timing is yours," he told her. "Based on how quickly you delivered Christmas designs that excited the entire executive suite, you could probably still leave right after the Project Forever Friends park festival. Your only obligation here will be to deliver the designs before you decide to leave Shelter Valley. And Brent is doubling what he's already paying you."

Her grin split her face so wide it hurt.

Until she noticed that Cole didn't look equally pleased.

"What's wrong?" she said, when she'd opened her mouth to give him an unequivocal yes to his offer. The new design consignment would give her the perfect excuse to remain in Shelter Valley for as long as it took for her to feel satisfied in leaving. Another week or two, or a month if that was how long it took.

Due to her last few phone calls with Savannah, she'd decided to remain in town while Sierra's Web did as thorough a search on Elite Paper and everyone associated with it as they legally could. She'd called her grandparents and her charity boards and let them all know, personally, that she might be extending her leave by another few weeks.

Cole, watching her, hadn't answered her question.

"Cole? What's going on?"

He cocked his head to the side. Smiled and, shaking his head, said, "Nothing."

"I don't get it."

"Get what? It's a great offer."

"Why are you lying to me?"

"I'm not." He grinned. "You don't need me to tell you that this is right up your alley, fits your time frame in terms of getting back to your grandparents, and Brent's showing you the respect you deserve with the money he's agreeing to pay you, too."

She got all of that. Gave Cole's words a cursory nod. "I meant with you. Something's wrong."

"We're at work."

And she got it. Like a slap in the face.

His problem wasn't with the deal on the table.

It was with her.

Personally.

And for that she was sorry.

Horribly sorry. Ready to cry, sorry.

But she still had to accept the offer.

It fit her purpose.

And whether her heart hurt or not, she was there for a clear reason.

Had turned over a rock that could expose harmful debris.

And needed to make sure that she did all she could to limit the fallout before she disappeared from the lives of Shelter Valley citizens forever.

Cole included.

If he was done with her before she was ready, that was a good thing, really.

Because if he'd been growing to need her like Lindsay Warren thought she needed him, she had no idea how she'd be able to hurt the man, by leaving, and live with herself.

She had to go. That much was unequivocal.

It would be best if she could get out as someone she could live with.

No matter how hard the tears were to hold back as she left Cole's office.

Because in the end, herself was all she was going to have.


Cole did not enjoy the birthday celebration for the elder Sam Montford. Everyone he knew was there. Beer flowed freely. Jokes were abundant. Food was plentiful and delicious. An outdoor trivia game with high-stakes prizes got his adrenaline up. And the sheriff and his wife had even brought a lovely woman—a newcomer to town—to meet everyone. He enjoyed conversing with her. Laughed out loud at her wit. And was not happy.

All night long, he wasn't happy.

Maybe because he'd rather have been in the smallest apartment in Shelter Valley having sex. But he didn't think so.

He'd been an ass with Lindsay in his office that day.

For what had seemed like, still seemed like, good reason. He was uncomfortable with his wayward thoughts where his relationship with her was concerned and needed to shut it down.

She was leaving. Wanted only a friendship with a fling attached. No hurt feelings.

And it was possible he had feelings trying to worm their way into something neither of them wanted.

Something that couldn't possibly work.

But Cole Bennet, hurting a woman?

He was the guy who soothed broken hearts.

There'd been no mistaking the flash of pain he'd seen in Lindsay's eyes that afternoon when he'd told her nothing was wrong.

Or rather, had inelegantly refused to tell her what *was* wrong. Him.

Her eyes had been moist, as though she'd been ready to cry.

And for what?

Because he'd thought his boss had called him into

his office to give him love life advice? Had suspected that Brent had offered a fabulous artist a deal that would greatly benefit Elite Paper, just to keep Lindsay in town for Cole's sake?

He stayed until the party broke up. Even managed to win himself a foursome at Phoenix's most elite, world-renowned golf course.

And then, before going home to face Lillie, he drove by Lindsay's complex. Turned in. Just to see if a light was on in her upstairs apartment.

The place was ablaze behind a lightly curtained window.

And without giving himself time to think about anything but facing his housemate without making things right, he dialed Lindsay's cell.

She answered on the first ring, before he even had a chance to second-guess himself, though he was pretty sure that wouldn't have happened.

"Can I come up?" No point in pretending he was calling after midnight just to chat.

"Not for sex." He smiled at her tone.

"Not for sex," he repeated, completely serious, even while he admired her grit.

"Then, yes."

She didn't question what he wanted. Was just opening her door to him, post rudeness, in the middle of the night, because he'd asked.

If Cole were the falling in love type, he might have just taken a tumble.

Heading upstairs in his dress shorts and loose short-sleeved button-down shirt, he was more thankful than ever that he'd left all thoughts of romantic love and happily-ever-after at the altar.

Nicky had not only given him undying friendship.

She'd given him the gift of peace of mind, too.

Lindsay didn't wait for Cole to knock. Still in the denim-and-silk skirt and blue shirt she'd worn to work that day—and to her dinner with Savannah—she flung open her door as soon as she heard Cole's step on her landing.

Then turned her back on him. After walking to her couch, she picked up the glass of wine she'd poured herself shortly before his call, and took a sip.

Allowing herself the false courage, the sustenance, she needed while he told her that he was ending things with her.

She was glad.

Didn't blame him.

And was set to make things easy on him by not getting all emotional or acting like a close friend who'd established some kind of bond over a period of weeks.

He made her laugh. She liked his dog. They'd had some great sex.

None of which denoted personal commitment.

"I discovered something about myself today that I didn't like."

His words threw her off-kilter. But not off course. He was feeling bad for dumping her?

He wasn't supposed to feel bad. She'd put a plan in motion. No one was supposed to get hurt. Except maybe herself. And she'd known that, taken that risk, going in. Wanting to serve him as he served others, coming up with some light response, she failed. Ended up with, "What did you discover?"

When he stood there, towering over her, she asked, "You want a beer?"

There was some of his left in her refrigerator and she sure wasn't going to drink it.

Glancing at his watch, he nodded.

And she couldn't keep her mouth shut on that one. "You got someplace to be?"

"I only drink one an hour when I'm driving."

Oh. He'd been at a dinner party. Had told her about it earlier in the week, which was why she'd chosen that night to meet Savannah.

Handing him the beer, she then plopped back down to the couch. Picked up her wine, more as a shield to hold in front of her than anything else.

But when he sat, looking so...un-Cole-like with his frown...her heart went out to him, and, taking another lesson from his ability to always be ready to offer comfort to others, she said, "What did you learn about yourself today?"

He'd obviously come to tell her. Helping him out was the decent thing to do.

"I think others feel sorry for me."

If she'd had wine in her mouth she'd have choked on that one. "Come again?"

"Apparently I have this clandestine view of everyone in town thinking I can't get a woman and they all want to do everything they can to get one for me."

He'd made a joke about the town's view of him that

first night, at the barbecue. Hadn't seemed the least bit bothered at the time.

More, he'd been aware and able to deflect any and all attempts with good cheer. She reminded him of the incident, and said, "You seemed to see their attempts at matchmaking as a sign of affection, not pity."

He nodded. Leaned back, flung an ankle up to rest over his knee, drawing her attention the short distance up his leg. He sipped. She swallowed.

Hard.

And, glancing at his still troubled expression, said, "Do you feel sorry for you?"

"Not at all." The way his brow cleared, the easy tone of voice, convinced her that he was right on that one.

"So what do you care what others think?"

Another shake of his head, another sip, and he looked her in the eye. "I'm not saying they think it," he told her. "I'm saying I think they think it."

If she'd had more to drink than her current half-filled glass, his words might have confused her. "You know you, and like you. But when you look at yourself through others' eyes, seeing yourself as they might see you…"

He nodded.

The distinction might appear small, but, having grown up in a world where appearances mattered, she got it.

"Now that you've realized you're doing it, change the channel," she told him something she'd learned young. "I used to think that kids resented me because my grandparents could give me more than a lot of kids…" She stopped. Caught herself. "…because they were older, you know. Already had careers and a house and enough of a savings to take me on fun vacations…"

She'd almost blown it. Fumbled with her save. But continued, because the point was valid. "Maybe they did, maybe they didn't. Maybe some kids thought that. Or one did. But I finally realized that I was worrying about something I'd not only never confirm—they'd probably lie if I asked them directly—and that wasn't going to change my reality at all. I knew me. And as long as I accept who I am, the opinions of others aren't going to matter."

The lesson had come much later than kids possibly resenting her because she'd been raised in overly abundant wealth. It had come when she'd taken charge of her own missing pieces and set out in search of her father. There she was, a woman who had everything, needing something else.

As long as no one got hurt in her search for more, she was not wrong to look.

Or something like that.

Cole's intent stare finally got through to her. He was telling her more than she'd taken in.

"That wasn't what was wrong, earlier, in your office, was it?"

He shook his head. She should have known. Cole was much too aware, confident and honest with himself not to have already figured out that others' opinions didn't matter in life's big picture.

"That part's coming now." She added.

He nodded. "You've thrown me off my mark." The

words fell flatly, with complete seriousness, between them. Landing with a thud.

"I don't know what to do with that," she said.

"I can't find my calm where you're concerned."

And that's why he was breaking things off with her.

The understanding didn't make the happening any easier, in that moment, as she sat there, all up in Lindsay Warren's fake life, alone with the hottest man she'd ever known.

One she liked even more as a person.

But then, she'd realized, going in, that her current plan wasn't going to be easy.

She just had to get it right.

## Chapter Fourteen

Cole finished off his beer. Needed another.

Stopping at Lindsay's, coming clean with her, had seemed like a good idea—pretty much mandatory if she'd see him—when he was outside in his SUV.

In her living room, getting words out seemed almost as hard as talking to Nicky in that swing on their wedding day had been.

Once he told her the truth, he was probably going to lose her.

But the truth was his only way. It kept him happy. Gave him peace. His confidence came from knowing he could handle anything life gave him as long as he was honest with himself and in his dealings with others.

"I can't find my calm because I'm emotionally attached to you."

Her face fell, just as he'd known it would. Mouth

open, she stared at him. Without a single hint of a happy gleam in her eye.

"I'm not in love, or anything," he quickly assured her. "And I'm definitely not looking for commitment or any long-term understanding."

She was frowning. He took that as better than the shock he'd been staring down seconds ago. And, so far, read no pity in her gaze.

There was nothing to be pitied. The ability to connect to people on an emotional level was one of life's greatest gifts. They'd just promised not to open that gift with each other.

"It just makes things messier," he finished, glad that he'd finally delivered what he'd come to say.

And could go home to Lillie with a clear conscience and get some rest.

Oh, and, "I apologize for my rudeness earlier today. I was still in the process of dealing with the realization that being around you throws me off my mark. I'm truly sorry."

There. Now he could rest.

Most particularly if he got out of there. Put a few miles' distance between himself and that incredible body calling out to him to make it feel good.

They'd agreed on a no sex visit.

"It makes things messier, how?" Her frown was still there, but she didn't seem to be in any hurry to get rid of him. Wasn't standing up. In fact, she'd leaned back farther into the couch. Took an actual sip from the glass she'd been holding up since he'd made his confession.

He shrugged. "Emotions are messy."

She nodded. Stared at him.

And he gave her what he figured she was waiting for. "It's going to sting a tad when you leave."

There. That was it.

The End of what he had to say.

Except, "You said no hurt feelings. I just broke that agreement."

She sat up then. Set her glass down. Stood up.

Dismissing him?

And he sat there. Looking up at her. "Are you prepared to look me in the eye and tell me that you won't feel a bit of disappointment when we end and you go back home?" It was like he was in mock court, arguing a case that didn't exist. When he'd been prepared just to close up shop and go home.

When she plopped back down, glanced over at him, he started to grin. Where the lightness came from, he couldn't say, but there it was.

Budding out of him as naturally as usual.

As though getting the truth out had brought him back in sync.

"If you want me to go, I will," he told her then. "And I won't contact you again, other than for Project Forever Friends business and work, but I have to tell you, I think making that choice would be a huge mistake."

Her lips trembled, but she didn't look away.

"A grave error," he said then, willing her to have the courage to take him on. To let herself have what she wanted while it was there for her.

"I don't want to hurt you."

"Too late. Whether it happens tonight, or at the end of the month, it's going to be hard."

"And the more memories we share, the more time we spend together, will make it harder."

He shrugged. "Maybe. Maybe not. We might mutually outgrow each other."

Her eye roll found an answering snort within him. "You know when you take yourself on a wonderful vacation, where you're going to have a blast, and not want to come home?" He threw the question out there, and continued without waiting for an answer to his hypothetical. "Just as, the whole time you're there, you know you have to go home. But you still go on vacation. Because that's life. You enjoy the great moments you're given, and even when one vacation is over, you still wake up every morning because you know that every day brings the possibility of more great moments to come."

"Kiss me."

He planned to. Had been hoping for the invitation since the moment he'd walked through her door, and felt as though he belonged there.

In her temporary home. Her temporary life.

But he didn't reach for her.

"You have anything else to say to me?" he asked. He knew women.

Whether she liked it or not, he knew her.

"You have me off my mark, too."

There it was. Grinning, he grabbed her up, right off the couch, into his arms, and headed to the bed.

"And I hate messy," she mumbled into his shoulder.

Cole laughed out loud at that.

And spent the next hour giving her what he knew she loved.

Great moments.

Lindsay had to rethink her plan. She didn't have to be in Shelter Valley for Sierra's Web to dive deep into Elite Paper and associates. Leaving town before Project Forever Friends was finished went completely against her grain, but in truth, everyone in town who'd jumped on board with her, including Cole and Mia Jones, was perfectly capable of bringing the project to a successful conclusion.

And the sooner she left, the sooner Cole could get over whatever hurt her leaving caused him. Since she'd messed up and couldn't avoid his pain, minimizing it was the next best option.

But…she'd be cutting his vacation short. When people looked back on their fun getaways, they didn't generally remember with much fondness the ones that were cut short.

She didn't want to leave him with the taste of ashes in his mouth.

Truth was, as the days went on, and she created to her heart's content, coexisted with her father from a distance, collected monies that more than doubled the fundraising goal, laughed with Cole and had inventive, soul-changing sex with him, too, she didn't want to leave at all.

Just like on vacation.

Because the reality was, her home, her life, herself— Lindsay Warren-Smythe—belonged in San Diego.

In the end, it was Savannah who clinched Lindsay's

decision to stay in town a few more weeks. Not only did the lawyer point out that she'd already signed paper-work in Cole's office on Friday afternoon to complete the Lindsay Warren Valentine line there on Elite Paper premises, but if Savannah and her Sierra's Web team came up with anything questionable within the com-pany, having Lindsay in-house could make a difference.

Not as a spy. But as someone who could ask ques-tions. Clear up misconceptions. So far, the team hadn't found anything, but with so many years, so many em-ployees and so many sites to search, they had a long way to go. And might need her.

She stayed because she had to finish what she'd started as efficiently, as quickly as possible. And the new plan was to give Cole the best vacation of his life.

One he'd look back on with the fondest memories. She let him call all the shots. It wasn't like Warren-Smythe could contribute money or ideas to give him fabulous, one-of-a-kind experiences. An impromptu flight to Rome in a private plane to share their favorite ham-and-onion dish authentically was out. But therapy visits with Lillie were a definite in. Making a warm fudge soufflé and then eating it off each other was in. A trip to Broadway to see his favorite play was out.

Skinny dipping in his built-in pool was a definite in. But spending all night together was out.

As with all vacations, there were boundaries. They just had to identify and manage them.

It all sounded good in her head. Let her get some nights of decent sleep as the last week of the extended past the initial two week fundraiser reached its halfway mark and she spent more time organizing booths than raising money for the celebration in the park that was still a week and a half away. With temperatures projected to be soaring up to 105 that day, she'd had to scramble to find huge outdoor open-front canvas "rooms" with misters, enough of them to cover the entire park. When the cost became an issue, putting the entire celebration at risk, she called Savannah and paid the entire bill herself, through Sierra's Web.

She had her plans. There was no stopping her.

Until she was stopped. Twice.

The first time was on the Monday prior to Saturday's park celebration. She'd stopped in at The Barbecue Pit to pick up dinner for her and Cole and Lillie—she and Cole were having a celebration day work session to plan out the main stage program times—and seated at the table by the door had been Brent and Emily Wilson and their three kids. With an instant sharp bolt to her heart, she'd put on her Warren-Smythe distant smile, and nodded. Only to have three of the five of them— Kaitlin and the two adults—all invite her to join them.

With a legitimate reason to decline—made more so by the young man behind the counter calling out her name with her to-go order ready—she was able to get herself out of the moment. But she'd carried it with her from that moment on. Because her heart had cried out for her to join them. Begged her to be able to do so.

And she knew she couldn't. Brent Wilson had made good. Sierra's Web had turned over rock after rock and found no alarming associations with the man. No evidence of money over and above what he'd make at

Elite Paper, no spending that sent up flags. The guy was maybe overprotective. A little too hands-on, if you didn't like that sort of thing.

He was also kind of a slob when it came to physically cleaning up his physical space. Or so she'd heard. He didn't always get his clothes in the hamper, and his desktop at work was always cluttered with papers.

But he was a good man. One she would not diminish with old scandal. News like hers could tear up that wonderful, healthy, loving family. Which would make her no better than he'd been when he'd run out on her and her mother.

She wouldn't be that father's daughter.

And couldn't be the current father's daughter, either.

Orphan that she was, Lindsay also couldn't live much longer in Brent Wilson's sphere. The ache to be a legitimate part of him was too acute.

But the firsthand knowledge she'd be taking with her, the pictures she'd stored in her heart and mind, were far more than she'd hoped for when she'd started her quest. She wasn't just Lindsay Warren-Smythe anymore. In her heart she was Lindsay Wilson Warren-Smythe.

And Ms. Bohemian had become Lindsay Wilson, not Lindsay Warren.

In her heart.

The second thing that stopped her, end of the line, forcing her to go, happened on the morning of the Project Forever Friends Celebration in the park.

Cole had picked her up at dawn as she had signage and a plethora of other supplies to load up in his much larger SUV. And when he'd taken a long minute inside her door to kiss her intimately, she'd swelled with a second of pure happiness.

If he'd asked her to run off with him and Lillie into the sunset, she might have done so.

Which scared her to death. No way were her own selfish needs going to rule her. Ever.

She chattered the entire three-mile drive to the park, including Lillie in her conversation as well as Cole, giving a rundown of jobs, of people they were meeting to help with various setups. Doing what she did best.

Filling her mind with details.

Lillie would have the run of the park. Sensing if she was needed—or just greeting people. Cole was in charge of main stage setup, and overseeing the installation of the large, portably covered, cooled horse corral.

She hit the ground with her own tasks at hand, unloading and distributing sign placement lists to the Boy Scout troop that had signed up for early morning volunteer duty. Next were the booth placement charts to off duty Shelter Valley Police deputies who were overseeing that setup. Martha Marks, Reverend Marks's wife, was in charge of verifying all permits as vendors came in. Ben Sanders, who'd come to Shelter Valley for an eight-years-late education and had fallen for his professor who was impersonating her deceased older sister, was in charge of electrical hookups.

Two air-conditioned bounce houses arrived right on schedule, and were being set up on opposite corners of the park. Traveling clowns were due midmorning, but their face-painting tent was already being populated with supplies.

The food trucks from local restaurants had just started pulling in, waiting in line for direction to their various predetermined parking spots, when Lindsay noticed Cole coming toward her with someone wearing the orange short-sleeved shirt with a logo denoting the tent company.

Even in the midst of all the cacophony, her stomach jumped at the sight of the big redheaded man she'd made love to twice the night before. He wasn't hers. She had to go.

But she'd known him. Had him to herself for several wonderful weeks. And, she hoped, a few nights more.

His gaze didn't meet hers as the two men approached, but there was so much going on, everyone had to stay incredibly focused to be ready for the celebration's ten in the morning start.

"We need a different kind of bolt down for the water corral," Cole said, wearing a frown as he stared at the clipboard the younger, much shorter, orange-shirted man held. "Horses are going to be here in an hour."

"Fine," Lindsay nodded, frowning, too, as she tried to ascertain the problem as quickly as possible in order to deliver whatever solution the duo was after.

"You have to sign for it, ma'am," the other man said, handing her the clipboard.

"I explained to him that I set up money-spending privileges for the project committee myself," Cole said, "but he insists that Cover All's bill is being paid for by Sierra's Web and only you have authorization to sign for additional costs."

Cole sounded harried. Frustrated.

And wasn't looking her way.

At all.

After grabbing the clipboard she signed, silently, and sent the men on their way to accomplish whatever her signature had just allowed in the short time allotted to them.

But she knew, as she watched Cole Bennet's retreating back, that her momentary lapse into Warren-Smythe, paying that bill, had just cost her any more time in Shelter Valley.

Cole would have no way of knowing that she'd paid that bill. But her own personal association with Sierra's Web—only known to Cole through Mia and Mariah's contacts—had clearly pinged off the radar of the sharp lawyer.

She could lie to him. Pretend that Mia or Mariah had put her in touch with the nationally renowned firm of experts and that Lindsay had convinced them to donate through her for the celebration tents. For a split second, the idea was tempting. Just to have one more night in his arms.

Except that the firm had already donated more than generously through Mia and Mariah.

And Lindsay wasn't going to sell her soul. Or sell him out, either.

She'd answer his questions as best as she could, without involving anyone else in town. Tell him who she was, without naming herself. And he'd be done with her.

Lindsay Warren had had her freedom.

And she'd reached the end of her road.

Vacation was over.

## Chapter Fifteen

Why did Lindsay Warren have a relationship with Sierra's Web? While the firm certainly did its share of pro bono work, only someone with substantial amounts of money, or law enforcement clout, could afford the fees.

So was Lindsay a pro bono client?

Cole had figured all along that she'd been hiding something from her past. Running from something, most likely.

But why, when she'd started Project Forever Friends, hadn't she mentioned, at least to him, that she was familiar with Sierra's Web? He'd heard Mia and Mariah talking to her about the firm, about two of the firm's partners, and she'd never once indicated that she'd ever heard of them before.

And they had her designated as a signee for their account?

It didn't add up.

Most certainly not if she was a pro bono case. No way would a firm with their reputation allow a struggling artist carte blanche with their finances.

Unless, since they weren't going to be on-site, they'd named her, the project chair, as designee? Based on her association with Mia and Mariah?

They'd have had the means to vet her first.

But Lindsay hadn't even looked at the bill she'd signed. She could have just spent a hundred thousand dollars of someone else's money and hadn't even thought to find out?

Because when he'd brought her the form to sign, she'd been swamped. And she trusted him.

The possibility presented itself, warming him up enough that he kept it on board and got back to work.

Keeping her in mind. And looking for sights of her as well. Two out of the next three times he looked around for a glance of her, he found Lillie, too.

Hanging close.

As the girl did when someone exhibited emotional stress.

Cole saw horses to their assigned tethering posts. He talked to Mia and Mariah. Joked with Kaitlin when she arrived with another trailer of horses.

And heard Lindsay's voice behind him, telling someone that their booth looked great. The sound stood out to him, as though it were a personal part of him.

Feeling the shock of it within him, he glanced around, saw Lindsay smiling as she walked down a row of booths, her hand resting lightly against Lillie's neck as the old girl kept pace.

And he knew.

He loved the woman.

All those years ago Lillie had prevented him from closing his heart off completely. And the old girl was showing him something else that was most likely obvious to her. When the time, the person, was right, open hearts loved.

"Cole?" Kaitlin's voice called out to him. Hearing her, he swung around, and saw that the teenager was watching Lindsay, too. "I tried to talk to her a little bit ago," Kaitlin was saying, "but she was too busy. Do you think, maybe, she'd take a look at some more of my drawings and, maybe, give me some pointers?"

He couldn't answer that. But he wanted to.

"From what I hear, she's been a real help at work, suggesting things, giving ideas to other artists, so I'm guessing, yeah, she probably would. But…" He scrunched up his nose at her. "I wouldn't ask today. She's got a lot on her shoulders, being new to town and all, and throwing, like, the biggest party of the year."

He heard his own words as he offered them.

Project Forever Friends had been entirely Lindsay's idea. Her energy had created a newsworthy event. For a town, a charity, she'd only just become acquainted with. She'd made it all look so fun, so easy, he'd lost sight of the emotional toll the project was exacting from her.

A newcomer to town.

"Cole?" The sound inside him, her voice, was repeating itself in his head as he knelt to give a final check to tent bindings attached to the corral fence. And then he saw the flip-flops.

Red with jewels.

They matched the red-and-white tie-dyed dress he'd been itching to shove his hand under on his front seat that morning.

Standing, he smiled at the woman who'd brought a much-needed breath of fresh air into his life. He didn't kid himself into thinking that she was staying in Shelter Valley.

Even with all of the hard work she'd put into a local cause, the mind-boggling party she was throwing.

But she was there at the moment and he was glad to see her.

"You okay?" he asked when she stood there, blinking up at him. "Did you need something?" He met her harried gaze with a long, calm look. He was there for her.

Always would be, whether she was there or not.

He loved her.

Not to be confused with being in love with her.

But...damn it felt good to be able to admit that he loved her.

"Just to say hi," she said then, smiling up at him. Seeming to find some measure of peace in the midst of chaos.

As though he did that for her.

"You're running an impressive show." He told her what he could. The whole love thing...not for anyone to know but him. And, of course, Lillie. "Half an hour until official festival opening and the place is already buzzing with fun and anticipation."

"It's this town," she explained. "Everyone pitching in. I've never seen anything like it."

Dare he hope that Shelter Valley was working its magic on her? Was it a fool's mission? Or love's benevolent energy pushing him?

Say she was a Sierra's Web pro bono case. They'd have taken her on because her problem wasn't easily solved, and was big enough, intense enough, that they felt she needed them to get the job done. That she couldn't likely do it without them.

He wanted to help.

Needed to help.

And, at that moment, it was crucial to her for him to stay focused. "What do you need?"

She stared up at him, her gaze melting into his. "A kiss?" Her response gave him another spin up the Ferris Wheel he always seemed to be riding with her.

"It's a date," he said. "Tonight. No matter how late this gig winds down." Booths and tents were to be vacated by ten. And would all be loaded up the next morning. Food trucks and the main stage were lights out at ten, too.

"Tonight," she told him, with one last long glance, before Greg Richards, the sheriff of Shelter Valley, called her away from him.

And as he watched her go, aware of his own list of responsibilities in her current endeavor, he vowed that he would find a way to help her trust him enough to let him share her personal life burdens as well.

As fabulous as Sierra's Web was, people who were

struggling, most particularly those who were running or hiding, needed personal support, too.

She'd picked him. And he wasn't going to let her down.

As a neighbor. A lover. And maybe, someday, as something much more than that.

With Lillie's blessing, anything was possible.

Lindsay had been unanimously selected by the Project Forever Friends committee to emcee the day's event, and she'd managed to get herself out of the high-profile limelight by agreeing to a short speech on behalf of the Project Forever Friends committee late that afternoon.

With Mia's help, there'd been press in from Phoenix for the monetary presentation to Forever Friends. Many of the journalists and influencers stayed for the presentation of awards as well. Lindsay waited until she was certain they were gone before heading to the mic. She'd made one huge mistake, paying for the tents herself. She couldn't afford a second one.

Standing in front of a crowd with her voice exploding over a speaker system was nothing new to Lindsay Warren-Smythe. But when Ms. Bohemian looked out over the crowd, lit by sunshine and enshrined by pure blue skies, she caught the eager face of Kaitlin Wilson turned up toward her and had to swallow.

"Good afternoon." She got the first words out. Had figured the brief thank-yous and praise for everyone in town would be a blip for her. And, seeing her father standing with Emily just behind their daughter, came up blank.

Had no teleprompter to lean on.

And there was Cole. Making his way up the crowd. Standing a good foot above most of them, his broad shoulders seeming to cover enough width for two people. "I just want to tell you all how amazing you are," she started in. Felt tears come up to clog her throat and smiled through her mandatory pause. Looked for Cole again, saw him standing just feet away from the front of the stage. With Lillie there, right beside him.

And knew, standing up there, in front of his entire tribe, with Lillie seeming to look right up at her, that she was in love with the man.

And his dog.

She loved them both. Her own private little family.

No matter what the future held for her, Cole and Lillie had shown her that she had the capability of loving deeply and completely.

And Shelter Valley—she'd found the missing pieces of herself there. In an older man's eyes. In the artwork of a thirteen-year-old girl. In a fifteen-year-old boy who still valued movie night with his parents. In the baby of the family who had more confidence than Lindsay figured she'd ever had. In the entire town of people who'd shown her the man her father really was.

"What you've done these past weeks," she started again, addressing the people who'd seemed prepared to patiently wait as long as it took for her to find her voice, "your monetary generosity, yes, but so much more, your genuine kindness toward each other, your energy when help is needed, your acceptance of strangers in your midst, your willingness to have fun… I'm thankful for all of it…"

She had to stop. Her throat was too tight for words and tears had sprung to her eyes. Turning, she handed the mic back to Mayor Becca Parsons, who was going to be announcing the magic act next up on stage.

And she made a beeline for the string of portable potties that had been brought in for the day. Letting Ms. Bohemian shed the tears that were refusing to be pushed back into their hole. And then, exiting to face the crowd with a Warren-Smythe smile on her face, she said a silent goodbye to the world in Shelter Valley and took the first steps back to her real life.

The second Lindsay shut herself in the front passenger seat of his SUV just after eleven that night, Cole felt the difference in her. He'd looked for her as soon as she'd left the stage earlier that afternoon, but had only made it to the side of the stage in time to see her back as she entered the restroom facility. He'd been roped into helping a local pediatric office bring in more boxes of the kid-sized colorful nutrition bars they were giving away and from there, he'd been needed back in the corral, helping to lift kids up into saddles for walks around the small area.

Lindsay had seemed fine when they'd shared a quick dinner of barbecued pork in rice bowls, though she'd been talking the entire time about how the event was going.

And at night's end, with all of the last-minute cleanup details, they'd barely spoken. Had just worked together, each fending off questions to which they both had the answers, to get the job done as quickly as possible.

He was tired. She had to be beat.

For a second, as she laid her head back against the seat, silent while he pulled out onto the city's main street, he'd told himself that he was just seeing another side to the woman he could happily spend a lifetime getting to know. She even wore exhaustion well.

"You want me to take you home?" he asked. She wouldn't spend the night. Her rule. Breaking it that night would be taking advantage.

Staring out the front windshield, she said, "No."

He glanced over. She didn't look at him. Didn't ask if he was too tired for the kiss date they'd made. He decided to like the fact that she felt comfortable enough not to worry about such things. That she knew him well enough to know he'd have told her if he had to call it a night sooner than they'd said they would.

And to figure that Lillie went straight to her love seat and lay down with her head on her paws when they got in the door because the girl had had such a long busy day.

He wanted to believe a lot of things.

But he didn't.

Lindsay's gaze as she sat on the edge of his couch and looked up at him was the glance of a stranger.

Not a tired lover.

Taking a seat on the opposite end of the couch, he felt like he was twenty-one again. Walking through the grass in his tux to his runaway bride sitting in a swing.

Lindsay hadn't left him at the altar.

She had associations with influential firms like Sierra's Web.

And he knew that he was not going to like what was coming.

As a powerful, wealthy woman Lindsay Warren-Smythe had learned in high school how to deliver bad news. With kids who'd wanted to use her. With dates who'd thought they could get more from her than she'd been willing to give.

With a teacher who'd once tried to get her to loan him some money.

You said what you had to say as quickly and succinctly as possible. And then you got out.

"I'm not a starving artist." She looked her target in the eye. He deserved that and so much more.

"Okay." Cole's reaction threw her. Where was the shock? The betrayal? Why did he seem...relieved?

"Okay." Did he know who she was?

And he hadn't told her?

He'd been leading her on the entire time she'd been in town?

Their relationship had been a hoax?

Ms. Bohemian flew into a tizzy inside her, and Lindsay had to take a second to calm herself down. To find herself again.

"It didn't make sense to me that, as talented as you are, you weren't earning more money than you let on."

Her mouth fell open. He thought her money came from her art?

She almost laughed at the irony in that pipe dream.

"I don't know why you thought you had to hide your wealth to work for Elite, and I feel like I need to know, and have a right to know why, but Lindsay, it's not the end of the world. You did a nice thing, paying for the cooling tents so today's celebration could go on. I'm guessing, after what you heard about Sierra's Web from Mia and Mariah, you reached out to them to help you donate anonymously, right?"

He'd handed her another chance. On what seemed to be a platter made of pure gold. If only she could tell him how much that meant to her.

And then lay her tired soul down on him, kiss him and go to sleep.

She was tempted.

So very very tempted.

Just for one more night.

"Right," she said, with a slow nod.

Saw the grin break out on his face.

And found no answering smile anywhere inside herself.

## Chapter Sixteen

Cole nearly laughed out loud, his relief was so palpable. He was just moving, to reach for Lindsay and get on with their kiss date, when she said, "And, not right."

Frowning, he stopped for a second, letting her continue with whatever she felt she had to tell him. He looked her in the eye, with the express purpose of letting her know her secrets were safe with him. And came up against an emptiness that completely shut him out.

What the hell?

"I used Sierra's Web to donate the money for the tents," she said, repeating the truth they'd already, to his immense relief, reached. "But I didn't hear about the firm from Mia and Mariah."

Oh.

Thoughts from that morning, right after she'd blindly

signed his form, bombarded him. With a twist. They'd just established that Lindsay was wealthy.

Which meant that she wasn't a pro bono client as he'd earlier concluded.

"I'm an heiress. By trade, I'm the chief fundraising officer of several charities, and I dabble in real estate as well."

"You're an artist," he said, sounding inane even to himself. "I've seen your work."

She nodded. "As a hobby."

"You're way more than a hobbyist, Lindsay…" He stopped. Shell-shocked. Not really comprehending the magnitude of what he was hearing. He watched her lips move. Heard the words come out.

And felt…blank.

Her chin trembled, and she almost smiled, before she said, "In my dreams, yes, I'm an artist. In real life, Lindsay Warren has a small apartment a couple of hours from home where she goes to hide out and create for weekend getaways, and, when she can sneak the time, she attends festivals to sell her work."

Feeling leaked inside the block of ice he'd become. Almost like he was absorbing the tears she wasn't shedding.

"And sometimes late at night, when I've come home from a full day of meetings and fancy meals, I let Lindsay Warren sneak off into the office and work on her website. It's a practical thing, I tell myself. It's not like I can hire someone to do it for me."

The way she referred to the woman he'd just that

day told himself he loved—as though she wasn't even real—seemed criminal to him.

Angered him.

For his sake, or hers, he couldn't tell.

Maybe for Lillie's.

The old girl…

It took a real shyster to get one over on Lillie.

Thankfully the beautiful collie was asleep and didn't have to be privy to the ugliness coming out into their living room.

"Who are you? What's your real name?"

"I can't say."

"Bull…" He finished the expletive with no shame.

And Lindsay, or whoever the hell she was, took it as though she deserved it.

And more.

Sucking in the lips he'd kissed all the way to heaven, she bit down, and then with an obvious deep breath said, "I told you that my father ran out on us. That he wasn't named on my birth certificate. And that I had no idea who he was. That was all true."

Too little to matter.

"Everything I've told you is true," she said then, as though, stranger that she was, she knew him well enough to read his mind.

Which pissed him off some more.

"What I didn't say," she continued as though he'd nodded encouragement, or was still at all open to anything she might want to impart, "is that Savannah Compton—the lawyer partner in Sierra's Web—and I became friends several years ago…"

He waved a hand to stop her. Like he cared who the heiress he'd mistaken for his lover palled around with.

"...she's the one who suggested that I look for my father," the powerful woman continued in spite of his signal to cease talking to him.

And she had his attention again. A flash of her pain when she'd talked about her parents hit him.

"Sierra's Web found him through one of those family DNA searches, and then, picking up a paper coffee cup he'd thrown away, they were able to get an official match. He's here in Shelter Valley. And while his past is shady—including the fact that he or one of his family members sold my mother the drugs that killed her—I needed to see him. To find the pieces of myself that were preventing me from being little more than a successful, dutiful robot."

Another bolt of sensation shot straight to his heart.

"Sierra's Web saw the ad Elite Paper had put out for an artist contractor, and I took that as a sign that I was meant to come to town and meet my father, without him knowing. I was going to get my answers, and get out without anyone getting hurt."

"You didn't intend to tell him who you were? To ask him why he left?" His curiosity won out over the anger for the moment. Just to get the facts.

A good lawyer knew it was all about the facts.

"Honestly, I don't know what I intended at first. It was all just this nebulous idea. And then I took one step toward making it happen and another, and suddenly I'm living in Shelter Valley, doing work that lights me up inside and...falling in love."

She looked at him then. The tears that pooled in her eyes, and fell, almost broke him to the point of hauling her into his arms.

But not quite.

If he hadn't handed her that clipboard that morning, she wouldn't be coming clean with him.

"You played me, like you did the rest of the town, so you could get what you needed."

It was one point in her favor that she didn't try to deny the accusation. "I never intended anyone to get hurt," she repeated. "I thought I'd be in and out, you know, like on vacation, you meet people, but you don't really get to know them. You're a piece of dust on their radar. Maybe a nice thought in the moment that fades to not remembering."

The ache in him grew. He didn't want to care for the stranger on his couch.

But he did.

And he thought of Nicky on that swing long ago.

Loving someone wasn't enough.

As much as he'd wanted it to be different, they hadn't fit.

"Who is he?"

"I can't say, Cole. He's got a good job here in town. A house and a wife. Kids. People seem to like him. He helps out like the rest of you."

Another horror struck. "He was there today?"

"Yes, but I didn't speak to him. He has no idea who I am and it needs to stay that way." The stranger was back, as though addressing a boardroom filled with men far more powerful, more wealthy than Cole ever wanted to be. "I've hurt you, and I will live with that for the rest of my life, but I can get out now and not hurt anyone else. Can you at least see that? If I say who I am, expose his past, who knows what it will do to his wife? His kids? His home in this town? Innocent people will be hurt. Children, Cole. I can't do that."

He didn't want to get it. God, he tried hard not to do so.

Just like with Nicky.

It was like the ten years he'd spent making certain that he didn't ever again feel that excruciating pain had never existed.

"I understand," he said, bowing his head and wishing he hadn't eaten so much for dinner.

The food wasn't sitting well in his gut.

Neither was the truth.

Whatever name had been given to the woman on his couch, he loved her far more than he'd ever loved Nicky. Loved her differently.

The forever kind.

But just like Nicky, he was going to have to let her go.

Lindsay needed to get up and leave. To pack her car and head to Phoenix that night. For that matter, she didn't even need to pack.

Lindsay Warren's six hangers and footwear would fit nicely in the seat beside her. The rest, the groceries, toiletries and cleaning supplies, she could just leave.

"I never lied to you, Cole," she said, instead of standing, the words tearing up out of her. "I swear to you, I never lied to you."

His head rose slowly and she braced for the anger, the hatred, the distaste that she'd see there. Instead, his red-curly-topped green-eyed gaze held hers steadily. Intense, searching...

She withstood the scrutiny. Would sit there the rest of the night if that's what it took.

In the midst of all her bad news, she'd just told him that she'd fallen in love. Had already told him that he turned her on like no other man ever had.

If she could just leave him with the truth of those words...

What?

He could spend the rest of his life pining for a woman he couldn't have?

Was she being selfish after all? Needing him to know that he was it for her? So that she could go away feeling like she meant something to him in return?

Weary from all the emotion, from life in a world where there was more than just fundraising and keeping up appearances, she thought again about climbing in her old yellow car and heading back to Phoenix.

To her real world—whether she liked it or not.

"Just tell me who he is." He finally broke the silence between them, but not the glance they shared.

"I can't." She shook her head. Lost eye contact. And felt bereft.

"Then at least tell me who you are."

The next shake of her head seemed to hurt every bone and muscle in her body. "He'd know the name.

And you can't come find me. Not unless you were willing to leave Shelter Valley and everyone you know and love here behind, without a forwarding address."

His nod broke her heart.

"This is why I didn't want to get involved with you," she told him then. "I let myself think that a vacation, short-term-only thing would be okay, because…you know…you hear about people having flings on vacation. And you were fully apprised of that part of the situation. And I couldn't seem to help myself. I've never been attracted to a guy like I am to you and… I'm sorry." She started to cry then. Ms. Bohemian tears, sobs and all. "I'm so sorry."

Cole's arms reached for her. But pulled back before they touched her body. And as bad as she hurt at the rejection, she knew he was right. Sucked up her pain and dried her tears.

They couldn't have what they wanted.

So they had to be done.

When he stood and grabbed his keys, she followed him wordlessly to the door.

A last glance back into his home showed her Lillie, on the couch, sleeping blissfully on.

The old girl was obviously done with her.

Lindsay Warren-Smythe wasn't even worthy of a goodbye.

As Cole led Lindsay out the door to his SUV, he was wracking his brain, trying to figure out who in town had a history of drugs in their past. Or a family member who'd sold them to a young girl in Southern California nearly three decades before.

Even more, who in Shelter Valley would abandon a young pregnant girl, and the resulting child as well?

Didn't matter if he'd made good…walking out on your family…never looking back…a person didn't get a "bye" on that one.

He buckled himself in. Started the car. Pulled out of his drive. "I know him, don't I?"

"Cole, don't."

He had to. He was seething. The life he wanted had almost been within reach, and was imploding right before his eyes.

The woman who loved him was hurting and he couldn't find a way to help her feel better.

"What kind of a guy abandons his family and then just goes on and has a great life?" He didn't even try to temper the bitterness in his voice.

Or to find something to smile about, either.

"Maybe he's spent his whole life making amends for wrong choices he'd made as a kid."

Stopped at a vacant corner, he stared at her, his heart open and seeping all over the front seat, not that it made a difference. "You're seriously making excuses for the dude?"

"He's my father, Cole."

Right. A part of her, she'd said earlier. The words hit home with a little more force as he sat there trying to right wrongs he had no control over.

But was somehow paying for.

As was she.

If they let the guy…

"But…" He started in and stopped when she shook her head.

"You and I…we did this…we started something when we both knew I had to leave…we agreed we wanted our great vacation even knowing it would have to come to an end. That man's wife, his children, the people who have befriended him, who value his friendship in return… I won't hurt them so that I can live on permanent vacation."

When she opened her mouth as though to say more, and then, closing it again, shook her head, his frustration grew. "What?"

"Shouldn't you go?" She nodded toward the stop sign.

He shrugged. "There's no one around." The sooner he pushed on the gas pedal, the sooner she'd be leaving his car for the last time. "What were you going to say?"

"It's not just the people here," she said then, sounding more distant even though he was buying a few more minutes in her presence. "My grandparents, and the slew of people who depend on me back home…they've been there for me my whole life, Cole. They need me. And Shelter Valley needs you."

She wasn't going to change her mind. There was nothing he could say to get her to stay. "I need you."

"I know, and I need you, too, but we've known each other a matter of weeks. And we're both strong people. We'll survive."

She was right, of course. They'd survive. He'd just be living with a permanent ache in his heart. Pushing the gas, he started slowly toward Main Street.

"At least tell me your real name." He cringed even as he said the words. Like some schoolboy begging for crumbs. "Just in case…"

His gut hit rock bottom as he pulled into her complex. "In case what?" she asked him.

How the hell did he know? "You know how to find me. What if I ever need to find you?"

"You could hire someone to try to find where Lindsay Warren, LLC leads, but I can already tell you that at this point, it will lead right back to Sierra's Web."

"How do you know I won't show up at one of Lindsay's shows?"

Her gaze lightened for a moment. His gut felt the reaction.

"I hope you don't." Her words belied the emotion he knew he'd just read in her expression. "Because saying goodbye to you a second time would be excruciating…"

Her voice broke. He heard the sob as she opened the door, slipped from the seat and walked out of his life.

Sitting there while he blinked back the unheard of moisture in his own eyes, Cole watched her climb the steps and unlock her front door, waiting for her to look back one last time.

She didn't.

She'd said her goodbyes.

And if he loved her at all, he had to honor her wishes and let her go.

## Chapter Seventeen

Lindsay watched from her window as Cole drove away. She grabbed her six hangers, her flip-flops, her Lindsay Warren laptop, threw her underthings in a bag, and with her purse already over her shoulder, headed out the door she hadn't closed completely behind her.

She'd email the file of valentine designs she'd completed that week as soon as she got to Phoenix. Stopped at the light waiting to enter the freeway ramp, she pushed her phone screen already set up for directions and sent a command for a voice text to Savannah.

She wasn't even on the freeway when her friend called her back, on speaker phone, insisting that Lindsay come to her place, not a hotel.

Warren-Smythe would never have done so. Not in her old life. She'd have checked into a quiet, elegant hotel and hidden out until morning.

With a more complete, albeit bruised self on board, Lindsay didn't argue with Savannah's request. She simply used her phone's voice command to change her destination.

And then, tearlessly, almost emotionlessly, she drove that hour and a half until her phone told her she'd arrived.

She didn't cry with Savannah, either. And though her friend gave her a concerned look or two, Savannah asked no questions. Instead, she gave Lindsay the space she needed to get on with her life. Starting with a hot cup of chamomile tea, and a welcoming guest room bed with soft sheets.

After sending her one email to Chief of Personnel at Elite Paper, attaching the designs for which he'd contracted her, along with a formal letter of resignation, she stripped off Lindsay Warren's park-dusty clothes, showered and went to bed. Surprisingly, Lindsay slept. Well. For several hours.

And when she awoke, it was almost as though the past month had been a dream. One that had changed her perspective of herself, certainly, had given her dimension where she'd been flat, but hadn't changed her daily life.

"Do you regret going?" Savannah asked her over coffee the next morning. "Did we make the wrong choice?"

An unequivocal yes, born from the depths of Ms. Bohemian's broken heart, didn't make it to Lindsay's lips. "No."

Because while she was hurting, sometimes to the point of being unable to draw air, the thought of never having known Cole, of not showing him how very desirable he was to women—at least one woman—and of not knowing of her own capacity to love, was worse.

And the abandoned girl in her was at peace, too.

What Brent Wilson did to her mother—and to baby her—was inexcusable. But the man had spent his life proving that there was more good than bad in him. He'd given his life over to blessing others.

And in so doing, he'd given his firstborn daughter something good to cling to, to take on, as the part of her that came from him. To feel less flawed in her darkest places.

She flew home to San Diego that same day and stopped to see her grandparents, telling them that, instead of going on a cruise, she'd spent some time with Savannah and helped with a horse therapy fundraiser. And she basked a bit in their pleasure, their pride in her, as she described the horse therapy program.

She was pleased with their ready offer to support, with time and money, her desire to add a pet therapy charity to her portfolio.

On Monday, she woke up and lived her normal life. She caught up on financials for her current list of charities, scheduled meetings, assessed needs and started planning events. That evening, she joined several dog rescue sites, putting Lindsay Warren's email on lists for notification of pets available, and she toyed with some ideas for a three-dimensional depiction of Lillie on the mountain path overlooking Shelter Valley.

She did what Lindsay Warren-Smythe had always

done. She kept busy. Contributed more to society than she took from it. Set goals, and then kept them.

The one major difference in her post-Shelter-Valley life was the time she carved out for Lindsay Warren. Thinking of Kaitlin Wilson, of the way Brent and Emily encouraged their daughter's talent, of Elite Paper and all the good that came from the company—and needing an outlet for the overabundance of emotion that threatened to overflow on her days—she let go of the lease on Lindsay Warren's small apartment. Instead, she set up a studio in her own home, and worked there before bed every single night.

And for several hours every weekend, too. She carved her creative time out specifically, and guarded it as though it were sacred.

As part of her plan to live a more honest, cohesive life, she showed some of her card designs to her grandparents, and refused to be discouraged when they gently told her that her pictures were nice and then changed the subject. She went home that night, searched out upcoming art shows and reserved space for Lindsay Warren at three of them, adding them to the website that very same night lest she let her practical side try to cheat her out of living as complete a life as she could.

As those first weeks passed, she didn't let herself think of Cole much. Or look at the photos she'd taken of him on her phone. But just as she knew the photos were there, she also took Cole's spirit with her everywhere she went. At some point, she realized that he was a part of her heart and would always be with her.

And found a measure of peace, and a smile, as she accepted the truth.

It was more difficult not to replay specific memories of Cole as she set up for her first art show, in Anaheim, early morning on a Saturday in September—exactly four weeks after the Project Forever Friends celebration. She watched people in charge of tents and thought of the moment when Cole brought her the clipboard with a form to sign that sealed the end of her time with him.

Blinking back tears, she pulled a big easel from the back of her luxury SUV, set it up in the front right corner of her booth and carefully unwrapped the large canvas that would sit on it. A collection of feathers and pebbles, some twigs, a couple of jewels, various glitters and acrylics that she'd priced outrageously too high to ever sell. The picture of Lillie on the mountain, overlooking Shelter Valley, was hers. She just needed to display it. To show the world that very private part of her heart in the only way she could claim it. Through her art.

Maybe because of Lillie, or maybe just because of Lindsay's more ardent dedication to the Ms. Bohemian part of herself, the show was a huge success. She sold out of most of her merchandise and took orders for everything from jewelry to three-dimensional dog portraits. Had she truly been living on a Lindsay Warren budget, she'd have made enough in one day for a month's worth of bills.

She was donating every bit of the money, through Sierra's Web, to Forever Friends.

"I'd like to buy this." The voice hit her in the gut as

she was packing up the empty easels, of various sizes, at show's end.

Turning, she paled, stood in the back of her booth, way behind her mostly empty table, and stared. Her arms wrapped around her, her hands running up and down over biceps left bare by the red-and-white spaghetti-strap dress she wore with her favorite red flip-flops.

Shivering, she looked around for the white sweater she'd had on that morning before the sun's heat took the chill out of the air.

Couldn't find it.

He'd asked what she'd do if he ever came to one of her shows.

She hadn't had an answer for him.

Still didn't.

"It's one hundred thousand dollars." Not finding her sweater, she blurted the outrageous price on the tag.

"I know."

"You don't have that kind of money."

"I do actually. Just need to cash in some of my Elite Paper stock. For now, I've got a home equity line of credit that will cover it." His green eyes brimmed with things he wasn't saying as he stood there in beige shorts and a loose-fitting short-sleeved black shirt.

In Anaheim. Not Shelter Valley.

Drooling inside, Lindsay had no idea what to do.

Lindsay Warren-Smythe had never been in such a situation.

There was no plan.

"It's not for sale."

"It says it is. The price tag's right here."

The advantage was all his. He'd known he was coming. "You've got her, Cole. That portrait is my only piece of Lillie." She admitted defeat.

Had no idea what she expected him to do with his victory, but bringing the portrait around the table to her was not it.

Because he handed it out to her, she took it. Figured he wanted her to wrap it up. And she would. Just as soon as she quit shaking so badly.

Setting the canvas down in the open hatch of her SUV, she stood with her back to the only person on earth who could make her come unglued.

And felt his arms wrap around her waist, pulling her back against his hardness, as his head lowered down to the side of her neck.

"Just let me hold you for a second, Lins. Let me smell your lavender-and-lilac scent. And I'll go."

She didn't want him to go!

He couldn't just show up there, and then leave her.

But he did.

He held on. Took some deep breaths as she closed her eyes, leaning back into his solid heat, savoring the seconds, and then, bracing her weight with his chest until she had her footing, he dropped his arms.

Turned.

And walked away.

The whole way to California Cole had been complacent about the trip. He'd needed to test the waters. To know, and let Lindsay know, that there was a way for them to see each other.

Or some such half-formed mostly innocuous justification.

Truth was, he'd been stalking Lindsay Warren's website just to ease the pain of having lost her. To keep himself sane late at night when it ate at him that he didn't even know her real name.

To hold her close in the only way available to him.

And when he'd seen the listing of new shows, it had been as though she'd been calling out to him. He'd had no choice but to go see her.

He'd purposely waited until Saturday morning of the show to head out from Shelter Valley. Had driven across the desert instead of flying so he'd be in total control of his timing. Had scheduled his showing up at her table at the end of the show. It had been the only respectful thing to do.

She was there for legitimate business and he had no right to interfere with that.

But her complete stupefaction when she'd seen him, her inability to rally, her capitulation to his bantering over the portrait of Lillie—they'd hit him hard.

Harder even than the first sight of that Lindsay Warren portrayal of his beloved canine companion.

She'd captured the essence of Lillie.

And as he'd stood there, holding her, he'd felt as though he'd stolen hers.

The woman loved him. Heart and soul. He knew what it had cost him when she'd left, but had given little thought to what her leaving had cost her.

Not just him, or a broken heart, but a father. A family of her own.

And she'd gone anyway.

In spite of the agonizing pain.

Because she wouldn't take her own happiness at the risk of ruining the lives of others.

His mind had grasped it all from the beginning.

But it hadn't been until he'd felt her collapse against him that he'd really understood. His being there wasn't a respite, a breath of air. It was making it harder for her to do what she had to do.

And for that, he'd be forever sorry.

Head high, back straight, Cole walked away from Lindsay's booth, from the art fair and out of her life.

He got in his SUV, set course for Shelter Valley and went home.

For her.

For good. He wouldn't be going back.

Because he was in love with her that completely.

And as bad as that hurt, he was still glad that he'd known her.

Cole had come!

Energized in a way she hadn't been since she'd left Shelter Valley, Lindsay was grinning the entire time she packed up the rest of her product and supplies, signed out and left the art fair.

She caught herself smiling as she drove south to San Diego, and grinned at herself in the mirror when she got home.

Cole had come to see her!

He was showing her that it wasn't over.

That while the answers weren't currently clear, at some point, in the future, they'd see each other again.

Maybe just at art shows. Spending nights in hotel rooms after each one.

At least until one or the other of them met someone who could become a permanent part of their life.

It wasn't ideal, but very little about life was perfect.

To the contrary, it was messy. Imperfect.

Which was why grabbing and cherishing those perfect moments made so much more sense.

Clearly Cole had already figured all that out.

In his totally Cole way, he was showing her a way to make it work.

Giving her time to get it.

She had no doubt he'd be back, maybe even at the following week's show.

Maybe the one after that.

Didn't matter which one he chose to appear at.

Next time, she'd be ready for him.

## *Chapter Eighteen*

Three Fridays after he'd been to see Lindsay, Cole turned
down Brent's invitation to movie night. The older man
hadn't said a word about Lindsay Warren since Cole had
delivered Lindsay's resignation letter, but after Cole's
overreaction to Brent's first ever invitation to bring a
guest to movie night, Brent had to have had a thought or
two about his mentee's state of heart.

The fact that Cole had done all he could to avoid
the man over the past month and a half, to give himself time to chill out from the whole thing, would have
Brent concerned, too.

He got it.

But for once, Shelter Valley's open arms, and the Wilson family's in particular, weren't going to help him.

If anything, Shelter Valley life, and the Wilsons' lives

in particular, were salt in his wound, as they showed him what he most wanted, but would likely never have.

And still, he didn't regret having known Lindsay. No matter how much it hurt, no way he'd have given up on the chance to have it all.

Even if just for such a short time.

As he was telling Lillie over his beer sitting on his back porch waiting for their steak to get done that Friday evening. Instead of movie night he was dining in with his girl, and drinking as much beer as it took to numb him a bit. He had nothing going in the morning.

Could sleep in.

And could afford one night a year of overconsumption.

Adding up the years without that one night he figured he'd accumulated eight of them. But, so far, was only planning to use up the one.

He told Lillie that, too.

Whether the girl got it or not, the straight calm look she gave him satisfied him enough to move on from that particular subject.

He'd just reached into his small outdoor refrigerator for his second can when Lillie jumped down and ran into the house, barking.

And his text pinged.

Glancing at his smartwatch as he opened the beer, he frowned.

Brent was there?

He turned down the heat on the steak, left his beer on the tiled outdoor counter and headed inside.

Whatever had happened, it had to be bad for Brent

to be showing up unannounced on movie night. He'd need Cole sober.

"What's up?" he asked, swinging his door wide the second he got to it.

Still in dress pants and short-sleeved shirt and tie, the older man's serious expression gave Cole pause, but calmed the panic shooting through him. If there'd been some kind of emergency, Brent would be more agitated.

"I'd like to talk to you, if you've got a minute." The successful businessman looked him in the eye, but without his usual confidence.

Had Brent done something wrong? No way he'd have been unfaithful to Emily. And the man didn't drink so a DUI was out.

Movie night wasn't happening so it must have been something substantial.

Feeling like he should be in lawyerly clothes, not the sweat shorts and T-shirt he'd pulled on when he got home, Cole said, "Of course." And showed Brent out to the misting patio.

With the vibes Brent was sending, fresh air and mountain views seemed better than being closed up in a living room.

Lillie followed Brent straight to a wooden rocker, and Cole watched as the older man's hand settled on the old girl's head, petting her slowly.

Brent glanced over at him, almost hesitantly, and said, "You haven't mentioned Lindsay Warren since she left…"

The name slammed down on Cole and he picked up his beer. Angry with himself for missing whatever nuance should have warned him that Brent's reluctance to speak was about Cole's reaction to what Brent was there to do, not about something Brent had already done.

After putting the name out there, Brent sat silent for a second, assessing Cole.

"I don't know what you want from me," Cole told him, banking his anger while he faced the man honestly. Brent deserved as much. "Yeah, I probably fell in love with her. I think she fell for me, too. But there were things pulling her back to San Diego and my life is here—"

"I have—"

When Brent interrupted, Cole shook his head and continued. "She told me before we ever started anything up that she probably wouldn't be staying. We agreed, mutually, to have a short-term thing and leave it at that."

Yeah, he was hurting. That only meant the time with Lindsay was real. Special.

And the fact that Cole had driven over twelve hours, round trip, to hold the woman for less than a minute and leave her…well, that was his business.

Brent didn't look any less…bothered.

In fact, if anything the lines marring his brow appeared to have grown.

Had Cole been that obvious in his heartache? Was everyone in town sharing the man's concern? Sending Brent to have a talk with him?

Pursing his lips, Brent nodded once, as though making a final decision—or reading Cole's mind—and then sat back, catching Cole's gaze, and holding it.

"I have…" he started again, and this time Cole didn't

interrupt. "I have a strong suspicion that I am the reason she left."

Cole heard the words. They made no sense.

"She was perfectly happy at Elite, Brent. If anything, having to give up the job working for you made it harder for her to leave."

Brent shook his head. Put a finger to the knot of his tie, but didn't loosen it. "I don't think she came to Shelter Valley just to take the job at Elite."

Cole froze. Mentally and physically.

"I think she was here to find me."

With a shaking hand, Cole set down his beer. Hard. Before he dropped it.

Brent was…had…drugs?

Brent?

Abandoned.

It didn't make sense. "Why on earth would you think that?" He finally got his thoughts in order. Asked the obvious question.

One he'd have come to immediately if he didn't know Lindsay's secrets.

Ones she'd told to no one else.

Had someone at Sierra's Web…?

He dismissed the thought before it even completed.

"Because I'm her father."

Cole's mouth dropped open.

His heart raged.

And Lillie jumped in his lap.

Heart pounding, Lindsay listened to the cell phone ring. Being stuck in traffic in LA on a Friday evening, on the way to a privately held small premiere, at five hundred a head, to raise money for a children's organization, didn't help her nerves any.

"Pick up," she implored, glancing at her in-dash screen to see that she'd indeed chosen to make the call from Lindsay Warren's cell phone, not her own.

Two shows. Cole hadn't shown up for either. She'd been battling with herself all week on what to do about that. Worried that she'd somehow given him the impression that his impromptu visit had been the wrong choice.

Needing him to at least know that she was willing to open that small door between them.

Traffic started to move.

Lindsay's call went to voice mail.

And she pushed to end the call without leaving a message.

Cole heard his phone. He'd left it in the kitchen after he'd collected the steak.

The steak.

It wasn't going to be any good.

At the moment, he wasn't sure what was good.

Brent was the man who'd been responsible for a young woman's death, and had abandoned his own daughter, too?

He couldn't wrap his mind around the facts Lindsay had given him and the man sitting there with the word *father* still fresh on his lips.

For a second he hated the guy. Wanted to stand up and spit on him.

For a second.

A flash of Lindsay, telling him she couldn't be responsible for ruining lives, hurting innocent people, passed before his eyes.

And with a sinking gut, he knew, not only what she'd meant, but that he'd been one of the people she'd been protecting.

In the next second, he was angry all over again.

She'd used him.

Elite Paper…she'd been there because Sierra's Web had told her Brent owned the company. It all fell into place.

Sickening, gut-wrenching place.

The barbecue. She'd seen how close he was to Brent.

She hadn't loved him.

She'd been using him to find out about her father.

Though…she'd never mentioned the man, or allowed talk of work when they were together…

Minutes had passed, long ones, since Brent had dropped his bombshell. *Because I'm her father.* Cole finally formed a coherent sentence. "Does Emily know?"

"Yes."

Okay. That felt right. And, "How is she?"

"Worried about me. And you, too."

"Me? Whatever for?"

The look Brent gave him had Cole glancing toward his beer, and taking a long sip. Before his thoughts turned back to Emily.

"She's worried about you? What about herself? Her kids? How could you do this to them?"

To any of them?

"Emily's known I got my high school girlfriend pregnant since our second date."

Cole stared. High school girlfriend? Lindsay hadn't mentioned that.

"Does she know about the drugs, too?"

Brent blinked and Cole said, "Lindsay told me why she was in town the night she left. She just wouldn't tell me her father's name. Or her own, either, for that matter."

Brent's nod, the way his eyes grew moist, the slight tilt at his lips, as though he'd almost smiled, drew Cole up short again.

"How long have you known?" he asked Brent then, to fill up the gaping hole that was growing wider by the second between the two.

"I suspected the first time I saw her. She looks so much like her mother, it's uncanny. That with the name, Lindsay Warren…" Brent broke off then, glancing at Cole and away.

"Her mother's name?"

"A portion of one of them," Brent conceded and Cole was frustrated all over again. Being denied the name of the woman a guy loved was not a pleasant thing.

The older man leaned forward, his elbows on his knees, and glanced up at Cole. "That and the fact that she was so talented, and willing to settle for what we'd originally offered as a starting position commission. It was enough to make me do some searching…"

"So how long have you known?" Cole asked again.

"The day I invited the two of you to movie night."

"And Emily?"

"Same time. She was with me when I got the results."

Cole waited to hear about divorce plans. "And the kids?" he asked when no other immediate bad news was forthcoming.

"Kyle and Kaitlin know I got a girl pregnant during high school. Kerby's a little young for that, yet."

"Do they know Lindsay is the product of that pregnancy?"

"No."

"Are you going to tell them?"

Brent's shrug left too many things left unsaid. Questions. Recriminations.

All things that were really none of Cole's business.

"Emily and I both think Lindsay deserves to know first."

Made sense to Cole.

"You love her," his onetime mentor said then.

Cole saw no point in denying the fact since he'd already blurted as much at the beginning of the conversation—before it had taken such a bizarre turn.

"And she loves you."

"I thought she did. Now I'm not so sure. She could have been using me to get to you."

With a raised brow, Brent pinned Cole with a glance he hadn't seen from the man in many years. At least not shooting in his direction. "You really think she'd do that?"

A woman who'd left town rather than expose the man who'd deserted her and had been partially responsible for her mother's death?

A woman who'd found a way to keep Cole from talking about the very man she'd come to investigate?

"No."

Brent's nod was slow. And continued over and over. Until the man finally said, "You think she'd be willing to come back, to be in your life, if I wasn't an issue?"

The point was moot. "You are an issue. There's no way Lindsay, or whatever her name is, would hurt your kids by exposing what you did."

Brent sat up at that. "I'm not proud of my part in what happened, Cole, but I don't keep secrets from my kids."

He'd kept them from Cole.

Who had parents of his own.

"You've kept them from the town."

Brent's frown came again. "Who here doesn't have a past?" he asked then. And started naming some of the people who'd come to town with pain and shame, and had been given second chances.

"I don't get how you could just walk out on your own child and never look back."

Brent's expression turned to stone. And then he sat forward, as though energy couldn't get out of him fast enough.

"She thinks I abandoned her?"

"Didn't you?"

"No."

"Then what happened?"

Brent shook his head. "I think she deserves to hear the truth, first, if that's possible," Brent said. "With Emily's blessing and encouragement, I'm planning to reach out to her, but, because of your feelings for her,

I wanted to speak with you before I did so. That's why we invited you over tonight. So we could speak with you together."

Cole was truly perplexed on that one. "Why should my feelings matter?"

"I thought you two broke up. Whether she instigated it or you did, either way, it could be awkward for you..." Brent told him.

And Cole's being settled a bit. He wasn't Brent's son, but the man still had his back.

"If you don't mind, I'd like to go get her, let her know you know who she is, and, if she wants to come back, I'll bring her to you," he said then, thinking a little of himself, but mostly of Lindsay. He'd have to wait for her next show, but having faced a lifetime of doing without, another week or two was a small price to pay.

"I'd be honored," Brent told Cole and then stood, holding out his hand.

Cole accepted the handshake with a full heart, and when Brent pulled him in for a hug, he gave that with gusto, too, before following Brent to the door.

"Tell Emily I said hello," he offered as the other man headed out.

Brent stopped, turned, said he'd do so and then added, "And, Cole? Her name really is Lindsay. The Warren is real, too."

And with that, he was gone.

Leaving Cole to sit with Lillie.

And dare to hope.

## Chapter Nineteen

Ringing woke Lindsay. A phone. Wrong ring.

Right ring.

Lindsay Warren's phone.

In the office.

At two in the morning?

Sliding out of her king-size bed, she made it down the hall and into the studio before the call ended. Had to jab twice with a shaking thumb to answer.

"Cole?"

"I looked at my phone. Saw a missed call from you…"

"And you decided to call me back at two in the morning?" She was smiling as she slid down the wall to her floor.

"I saw the missed call," he said again, as if that explained things. Which it did. "I thought I'd have to wait for another show, but you haven't posted any, and then I see you called."

And he'd called back in the middle of the night.

She'd been elated.

And…

What were they doing? Prolonging the heartbreak by giving in to weakness? She'd had a long, boring premiere to sit through, that night. Way too much time in the dark to think.

"I need to see you, Lindsay," his voice sounded different. Totally serious. "I know who your father is, and I'm in San Diego. I just need an address."

"What!" She stood up. "Wait, you're here?"

Other than the city, he didn't know how to find her. Which meant he didn't know her real identity.

"I've been driving all night."

So, he hadn't *just* noticed her missed call.

And that was the thought she landed on?

He couldn't know her father's identity—no one knew but her and Sierra's Web, and she couldn't have Cole showing up in Warren-Smythe's world, either.

But she gave him the address of a furnished condo she owned. One she kept to house out-of-town business associates on occasion. Told him to meet her there in an hour.

And then jumped in the shower.

She'd been wrong to call him. To give him hope.

She had to end things, once and for all.

Cole was waiting in the parking lot when Lindsay's smart little Porsche pulled in. He'd been watching for the SUV he'd seen her loading in Anaheim. Was glad he'd taken the time to pull on dress pants and shirt before leaving home, when he saw her pants and cropped short jacket.

He'd chosen his professional gear for moral support. Jeans didn't seem appropriate to the moment. But wasn't sure her choice of outfit boded well for him.

Nor did her greeting in the parking lot. Kind, but all business.

Because he was close to the man who'd abandoned her?

But she'd known that before she'd left town. He'd apparently been the only key player in the dark.

They weren't even fully inside the door of the luxury unit before she flipped on a light and turned to Cole. "Look… I was wrong to call you, and I'm sorry, but you can't…"

"Brent Wilson plans to reach out to you," he interrupted. Because when he looked in her eyes, he felt her panic. "I asked him to let me come get you and bring you to him. Because if you don't want to see him, I'm going to make certain that he leaves you alone."

The words were just there.

And complete truth.

"Brent…" Mouth open, eyes wide, she dropped down to a couch, the closest piece of furniture in the vicinity. "He knows?"

Cole took a deep breath. So, it was true. A part of him had been expecting differently…

Joining her on the couch, he left plenty of distance

between them. "He said you're the spitting image of your mother."

"When?" She shook her head. "When? How long have you…"

"Tonight," he told her, wanting to hold her, not for sex, but so that she knew she wasn't alone.

"And you…you're okay with it?"

If it was possible, Cole fell in love all over again. So Lindsay, thinking of others when her own world was in crisis. And it dawned on him. Maybe that was why she always had others on her mind. So she didn't have to feel the holes in her own life.

"I'm not overly fond of him at the moment, but I love the guy." He had to be honest with her.

His response seemed to ease her somewhat. The lines on her face faded. Only to come again. "He really wants to see me?"

Cole heard the hope there. And saw the anguish in her eyes, too.

"He says he didn't abandon you, Lindsay. Had a shocked expression on his face when I accused him of doing so."

Her snort was so unlike the woman he knew, as was the bitterness in her gaze, and Cole was back in lawyer mode, ready to keep his mentor from ever seeing her. "What else did he say?" she asked.

"That you deserved to hear the truth before he told me or anyone else."

"Did you tell him I know about the drugs? Did he try to get out of that, too?"

"We didn't discuss details, but when I asked him if Emily knew about the drugs, he said she did."

"Emily? She knows?"

"He told her on their second date that he'd gotten his high school girlfriend pregnant."

"High school?" Lindsay shook her head. "They'd just met, the summer after she graduated…"

Cole's shrug felt weak. He didn't have enough to ease her pain. Except, "I'll take you to him, if you want to go," he said. "We can be there by midmorning, and I'll have you back here by tomorrow night."

"You need to sleep, Cole."

Did that mean she was going with him?

Oddly enough, he didn't feel at all tired, and told her so. Mostly he didn't want her to be alone. But when she offered to let him stay at the condo, and meet him back there in a few hours, he had to let her go.

She texted him a few minutes later, as he'd asked, to let him know she'd made it home.

But didn't say anything else.

No "I love you, it's good to see you," or "thank you." Not even "good-night."


Thankfully Cole had shown up on a weekend, and Lindsay was able to excuse herself from the mostly social functions she'd been scheduled to attend. As she dressed on Saturday, midmorning, she didn't spend time thinking about what a daughter wore to meet her father for the first time. She and Brent Wilson had already met.

She dressed like the confident, successful, independently wealthy businesswoman she'd become of her own accord. In expensively tailored gray pants, a cream silk camisole and the matching cropped jacket that went with the pants. And slip-on heels that cost far too much. She wore her two-thousand-dollar gold hoop earrings from her grandfather in one of her ears' three piercings. And filled the other two with similarly expensive, if smaller, gold hoops.

And for the six hours across the desert she held her silence, other than to respond to Cole Bennet's small talk. He was her ride. Brent Wilson's protégé. A member of the man's family.

He couldn't be her rock.

Or even a friend.

When he pulled onto Brent's street, the ice around her cracked for a moment. "We're going to his house? What about his kids and…"

"The older two know Brent had a child, but they don't know it's you," Cole said, shocking her. Unnerving her.

Shattering another layer of the shields she needed to get through the meeting and make it home in one piece.

"But they're all with Emily, watching Kaitlin in a rodeo being hosted at Homestead Ranch."

Mia Jones's place. She'd liked Mia.

They hadn't even pulled fully into the drive when she saw Brent Wilson come out the front door of the house and stand on the massive porch.

As though he owned the world.

The bitter thought crept through, shoring her up for the potential lies that lay ahead. It didn't take a genius to figure out that if the man had figured out she knew who he was, he'd know she could choose to inflict damage upon him any time she chose. He could offer to buy her silence, but he'd know that she didn't need his money.

She wondered, as she exited Cole's SUV, what he'd try to offer to get her to go quietly away. What he thought he had that she'd want.

Then she noticed that Cole wasn't getting out of the vehicle, and stopped to glance at him through her still-open door.

"What are you doing?"

"Leaving you to meet with him in private."

"If you aren't coming, I'm not going," she stated without thought. Ms. Bohemian to the rescue. A new thing.

Cole got out.

And Warren-Smythe was back in action.

Until she climbed the steps up the porch and saw the intensity, the welling tears, the trembling lips on the face of the man she'd come there to hate.

"They told me you didn't make it," the man blurted, any resemblance to the nurturing, calm man she'd known Brent Wilson to be just…gone. "That you were stillborn. I never would have taken the agreement. I swear to God, Lindsay, I would have stayed—I'd have taken whatever punishment they wanted to hand out, if I'd known you were alive."

*They?* Who? What in the hell was the man babbling about?

And why were there tears in her eyes? Blurring her

vision when she'd never needed to see more clearly in her life.

She shook her head. Ready to call him on his lies, but couldn't get words up through her throat.

"I was trying to stop him from selling to her. I'd had no idea...she wanted to be an artist, not a philanthropist, but she couldn't stand up to her parents. We met in art class and while I had talent, she was worlds above me. She was such a sensitive, sweet woman, with so much to offer, but she didn't have the strength to oppose her mother and father. She didn't even tell them about me until she could no longer hide the pregnancy. Then when they refused to let me see her..."

The man fell to a chair on the porch, as though broken, and Lindsay sat, too. In the chair across from him. Looking up to Cole.

A chair by Brent. A chair by her.

His choice.

He sat by her.

It mattered. She couldn't think why.

"I don't get it," she said. "You found out Mom was pregnant. You left. She had me and then got back on the drugs you and your brother had been selling to her. End of story."

She didn't need his emotion. His regret.

She needed truth.

"I'd known she was pregnant for months before she told her parents. I wanted to marry her." The man was looking her right in the eye. No wavering. "Her parents told her they'd cut her off if she didn't end things with me. We had no health insurance. My home life wasn't good. Mom was gone as much as she was there. My brother was dealing drugs. I told her we had to do what her parents wanted. Just until I could get my diploma and get a job. Next thing I know, her parents' lawyer calls to tell me the baby is gone."

She shook her head. Physically and mentally. Didn't want to believe a word of what he was saying.

Wasn't willing to give him any trust at all.

But hearing some sense in his story, too. What he was describing...sounded exactly like things her grandparents would have done. Down to the baby being "gone." Leading him to believe one thing, when it could have simply meant that they'd taken her away from the city for a while.

They'd have had the best of intentions.

They lived in a world where order and rules didn't change a lot. Where there was only one way to do the right thing.

But she had questions. A ton of them.

"I was a mess, drinking too much," Brent Wilson continued before she could voice a single thought. "And one night my brother lets me know that I'm wasting my energy, hurting over your mother like I was. He said that she was out partying, getting high. I refused to believe him. He showed me a picture of her with some of her wealthy friends. My brother's *clients*. I tried to reach her, but no one would let me near her. Then one night, I hear my brother on the phone. He's getting ready to make a drop-off in her neighborhood. He needs to borrow my car. I won't let him. He fights me for the keys—I got a busted lip, and he got my car. I jumped in as he was leaving, thinking I'd finally found a way to get to her. Instead, he gets busted, and I did, too, right along with him."

As though watching a train wreck, a horrible one, with people screaming, Lindsay sat there, listening. Cole's hand touched her. And then, something wet.

A nose?

Looking down, she saw Lillie. And the doggy door not far from Brent. Of course, whenever Cole left town, Lillie stayed with the Wilsons.

The fact was an easy one to focus on. Truth.

Lillie's face would never lie to her.

She looked at the dog, petting her, as Brent continued. "The Warren-Smythes knew that I wasn't a dealer. They talked to the sheriff, the prosecutor, and I was told that all charges against me would be dropped if I left town and never attempted to contact them or your mother again. If I tried to reach out to her, I'd be going straight to jail. They swore she was going into rehab, and then on to college."

The man's voice drifted off. She heard it go. Appreciated the silence.

Until it started to hurt too much. Lindsay looked up. Met the brown-eyed gaze with the lighter ring around the outside. And couldn't let go.

"I took the deal, Lindsay, but I swear to God, I didn't know you were alive. I would never, ever, ever have left if I knew you were alive."

Lindsay didn't believe in many things she couldn't see, as fact, on paper.

But in that moment, she believed her father.

And quietly told him so.

* * *

Cole should have felt superfluous over the next hour as Lindsay and Brent, father and daughter, talked. About hard things. And easier ones.

Brent wanted Lindsay to listen to her artist's soul, to pursue the talent her mother had given her. Lindsay, like her mother, felt obligated to her grandparents.

And Cole began to see that it hadn't been only Brent Wilson keeping him and Lindsay apart. She was a Warren-Smythe, as her mother had been. Raised to standards that were a part of her.

And not of him.

Brent asked her to stay in town for the weekend, and she demurred. Saying that she had to get home, had commitments, but left his house with a promise to come back.

Soon.

And after climbing down the porch steps to the ground, went back up again to give the man a hug. A long one.

Hopefully, a healing one.

"You want to head straight back?" Cole asked, bracing himself as he turned his SUV around and headed down Brent's driveway. He caught a glimpse of the older man in the rearview mirror, standing alone on his porch, looking somewhat lost and alone, and wondered if the image was a mirror of what his own life would be.

"You want me to head straight back?" Lindsay asked, staring over at him in a way that confused him.

Like he was missing something. Too far gone, too emotionally involved, to properly ascertain the entirety of the situation, he gave her the truth. "Hell no. I want you to come home with me and spend the weekend. We'd have to leave Lillie with the Wilsons because if they knew you were staying, they'd want you to come back, and I don't want you to feel obligated to go back there right away, but..."

Her grin took his breath—and the rest of whatever else he'd been going to say.

"Hell no works for me," she said, and crossed one elegant leg over the other, leaving him in no doubt what she was feeling where.

Lindsay didn't want any more knowledge. Or spoken truths.

She needed things that went deeper than understanding. And let Cole know what she hungered for in every physical way she could the second they got inside his house.

What it all meant, where it could lead, she didn't know. She wasn't the maker of the universe. Had no control over fate.

But she knew how to show the man she loved how very much she needed him.

They made love without questions. Without promises.

And then did it again with words of love. Of longing. Of having missed each other.

Sometime after dark they made it out to his kitchen for sandwiches, and sat out on the porch, in the dark, eating them.

And Lindsay longed for Lillie. For the dog's steady presence. Her knowledge and assurance.

"I'm thinking Lillie is where she needs to be tonight," she said aloud, as the thought occurred to her. "Brent needs her more than we do right now."

The man had his wife. His kids. His whole great life.

But he'd lost twenty-eight years with his firstborn child.

Twenty-eight years he'd never get back.

"I want you to stay." Cole's words split open the cocoon they'd been nestling in all day.

She had a life. Obligations.

Her grandparents.

Who'd…with all the best intent…stolen her father from her. And her from him. Stolen him from her mother, too. Along with her mother's artist's soul.

Lindsay could relate to that part with a vengeance. "I need some time."

"I was thinking maybe I work from home half the time, you know, the weeks I'm in San Diego, and you do the same, when we're in Shelter Valley."

The idea of it…what a dream!

But practically speaking… "What about when we have kids? They can't be split between two states, two schools, two sets of friends…"

She heard her words and stopped.

He hadn't even asked her to marry him and she was birthing babies?

They'd known each other less than three months.

"By the time we get pregnant, add nine months until the birth, then another three or four years until we're thinking about preschool… I'd say that'd give your grandparents enough time to come around. And either move to Shelter Valley, or be willing to visit often…"

Her heart soared. Of its own accord, the damned thing just took off. "What if I want to live in San Diego?" she asked, just because…she liked teasing him.

She didn't need to hear his response. She already knew it. But she listened anyway, as he said, "Then I guess Elite Paper would have to pay for my private jet to and from work, and we'd be doing a lot of visiting our home here on weekends and during the summer."

"A private jet, huh?" She was smiling full out.

"Just think—we could get one with a hot tub and king-size bed and spend the flight time…"

Lindsay cut off whatever else he was going to say with a kiss so hungry it made her cry. And when he picked her up, with their lips still joined, and carried her to his bed, she didn't even try to stop the flow of tears.

"I love you, Cole Bennet," she said, looking him in the eye as he set her down against his pillows.

"And I love you, Lindsay…Warren-Smythe, is it?" He grinned at her.

She laughed out loud.

And knew, no matter what challenges that came their way—and they could count on them coming—they'd be met with laughter and love.

Joining her on the bed, Cole held himself up on one elbow, met her gaze and said, "Lindsay, will you ma…"

With a finger to his lips, she silenced him.

"Don't you think we should wait for Lillie to come

home before you do that? The girl would be hurt if she didn't get to give her blessing."

His smile lit up her heart. Her whole world.

And when, instead of proposing, he kissed her, she silently issued the answer to the question he hadn't yet asked.

She gave him her love. Her heart. Her always.

\* \* \* \* \*

*You'll love other books in*
*Tara Taylor Quinn's Sierra's Web miniseries:*

His Lost and Found Family
Reluctant Roommates
Tracking His Secret Child
Her Best Friend's Baby
Cold Case Sheriff
The Bounty Hunter's Baby Search
On the Run with His Bodyguard
Their Secret Twins
Not Without Her Child
A Firefighter's Hidden Truth

SPECIAL EXCERPT FROM

**HARLEQUIN**
**SPECIAL**
EDITION

*With the help of an unusual Cupid, can two
friends who've known each other forever
take a chance on love?*

*Read on for a sneak preview of
Matchmaker on the Ranch
by Marie Ferrarella.*

## Chapter One

Yesterday had been one of those extremely long days for Rosemary Robertson. She was affectionately known to her family and friends as "Roe," as well as the "youngest triplet" to her sisters because she had been the last one of the trio to make her appearance that fateful evening that her widowed mother had given birth.

Now, exhausted beyond words, Roe had no recollection of even climbing into her bed. One minute she was making her way into her small bedroom, the next minute she had made contact with her pillow.

She was sound asleep probably before her head had hit her pillow.

She didn't even remember lying down. The one thing she knew was that she certainly hadn't bothered getting undressed. The allure of the double bed had seductively called to her, and the next thing she knew was sleep. It was a good thing that her two dogs, Kingston and Lucy, had stayed on the floor; otherwise, she could have very well flattened one of them, if not both, as her body made contact with the bed.

But after living with their mistress for a number of years, the Bichon Frisé and the petite German shepherd had developed survival instincts when it came to being around the town's veterinarian.

The dogs had also developed certain habits when it came to living with their mistress.

One of these habits involved waking her up at a certain time in the morning. The way her dogs went about this was to lick her face—vigorously—until she would finally open her eyes and respond to them.

And that was exactly the way Roe woke up the next morning, having her face bathed by pink tongues, one very small tongue, one rather large tongue, both of which were moving madly along her cheeks. She had fallen asleep on her back, and each dog had picked out a side, anointing her until her eyelashes finally began to flicker and then, at long last, opened.

Roe groaned, shifting on the bed. She did her best to attempt to wave the dogs away from her face.

"Oh come on, guys, just give me five more minutes. Please." She sighed deeply and attempted to wave the dogs away again, but their licking only grew more pronounced and frantic. Roe gave up. "Okay, okay, I'm up, I'm up," she told the dogs, struggling into an upright position.

With another deep sigh, Roe scrubbed her hands over

her now very damp face, doing her very best to try to pull herself together.

It was a slow process, but she was getting there.

Finally fully awake, she looked from one dog to the other. "You know, if you don't change your tunes, I can always find a nice home for you two. What do you think of that?" she asked, attempting to pin the dogs down with a look.

The pets apparently weren't buying it. Kingston, clearly the leader despite his size, began licking her face again and this time, Roe gave up and just laughed at her pets.

"Okay, okay, I know where this is going. Time for your breakfast," she told the dogs. "But first you're going to have to let me get up out of bed." As if by magic—she had trained the two dogs relentlessly when it came to obedience—Kingston and Lucy retreated from her bed. "That's better," she said, praising them.

Roe swung her legs off the bed, searching around with her toes for her shoes. She usually wore boots all day, then pulled them off the moment she walked in the front door and put on her shoes in their place.

Finding her shoes, she slipped into them and then stood up.

"Okay, let's go see about that breakfast," she told the dogs.

Her furry fan club all but hopped around her in a yappy circle, not exactly getting underfoot, but not exactly steering clear of her, either.

Roe made her way into the kitchen and began preparing two bowls of food for the dogs. The bowls each

had boiled chicken thighs, a tablespoon of pureed pumpkin sauce, a sprinkling of cheddar cheese scattered on
top and just enough dog food to make it an all-around
meal for the pets.

Once done, she set the bowls down on the floor and
watched the dogs go at it as if they had been starved for
days instead of fed midday yesterday when her neighbor had come in to leave dishes for her pets that Roe
had prepared.

Roe always got a kick out of the fact that Kingston
cleared his bowl much faster than Lucy did, despite
their difference in size.

"No picky eaters here," Roe declared happily. They
had all but cleared their bowls completely in less time
than it had taken her to put the meals together. "Well, I
hope you enjoyed that because you're not getting anything more until I get home tonight," she told them as
she filled their water bowls. "With any luck, today won't
be anything like it was yesterday. I hardly got a chance
to take two breaths in succession."

As she spoke, Kingston cocked his head first one
way, then the other. The dog she had found stumbling
around town one morning eight years ago had become
attached to her almost instantly. He'd had a large,
fresh gash in his rear right leg at the time. She initially
thought she might have to amputate it because it looked
as if a serious infection was swiftly spreading through
the injured limb.

By working diligently and relentlessly, Roe had managed to save his leg and keep the infection from spread-

ing until she was finally able to eradicate it. But it had been touch and go there for a while.

Initially, she had taken Kingston home to watch over him until he got well. Slowly, eventually, her home became his home.

Permanently.

Lucy had turned up on her doorstep a year and a half after that. If she had ever harbored any doubts about her ability to care for animals, Lucy quickly cured her of them. The frightened dog had been easily won over by her. Roe came to the happy conclusion that she had an affinity not just for caring for animals, but for curing them as well.

She stood for a moment now, just looking at the two dogs that had added so much meaning to her life. Roe could feel her happiness radiating inside of her.

It took effort to draw herself away the pets, but she managed.

The rest of the day was waiting for her to get started.

Roe had just gotten out of the shower and hadn't even had a chance to dry off yet when her cell phone began ringing. She shook her head as, still dripping, she glanced over at the phone she had left on the side of the bathroom sink.

"Looks like it's going to be another wonderful, chockful-of-patients day," Roe murmured to herself.

Grabbing her bathrobe with one hand, she picked up her phone with the other and put it on speaker. She rested it on the sink as she punched her arms through her bathrobe sleeves. She wanted to at least begin the process of absorbing the dampness from her body, not to mention having something on to cover her.

"This is Dr. Robertson," she told the caller. "How can I help you?" Roe asked, leaning over the receiver as she raised her voice to a more audible level.

"You could try picking up your phone when I call," the voice on the other end said.

A lot of people who interacted with them said that not only did the three Robertson sisters look alike, they also sounded alike as well.

But those who *really* knew the sisters claimed that they could actually tell their voices apart.

"I was in the shower, Riley. What's up?" Roe asked as she quickly toweled her hair dry with one hand. "And although I know I don't have to tell you this, talk fast. I have an early morning appointment with a rancher."

"Hmm. Business or pleasure?" Riley asked. Roe caught the interested note in her sister's voice, but that could just be because Riley was getting married and she was interested in everyone's situation.

Kingston was watching attentively as Roe swiftly finished drying herself off, then stripped off the now-soggy bathrobe.

"Both," Roe answered her sister matter-of-factly. "My business always gives me pleasure."

"Nice to hear. And how do you feel about weddings?" Riley asked her, deliberately sounding vague.

Roe closed her eyes as she hit her forehead with the flat of her hand. "Oh God, the rehearsal. I forgot all about the rehearsal," she cried. She was supposed to be there later today, after her appointment. "I am so sorry."

"Well, despite the fact that I have a spare sister I can always turn to, I do forgive you. But only because I am so very magnanimous and kindhearted," Riley told Roe. "And it's not like you haven't been to a wedding before and have no idea what to expect or do," she added. And then Riley changed her tone as concern entered her voice. "You sound really tired, Roe. Is everything all right on your end?"

"Honestly?" Roe asked, momentarily at a loss.

"No, lie to me," Riley answered cryptically. "Of course honestly."

Roe sighed, thinking of the possible threat that might lay ahead when it came to the cattle ranch she had been to the other day. "I'm not sure yet, but that's not anything for you to concern yourself about." She grinned as she made her way into her bedroom, carrying her phone with her. "You have a wedding to plan and nothing else should matter right now.

"Speaking of which," Roe said, continuing her train of thought as she opened her closet and took out fresh clothes for the day, debating whether to bring a second set with her to change into later. She decided it wouldn't hurt to toss them into the trunk, just in case. "Are you sure you want me to be your maid of honor? People might get confused. Especially since you're going to have Raegan as your matron of honor."

Riley laughed, dismissing her sister's concerns. "Anyone who doesn't know that I have two sisters who are mirror images of me really doesn't concern me because they're relatively strangers," she informed Roe. "Just as long as you and Raegan don't get your roles confused, that's all that counts," Riley teased, then went on to clarify the roles. "You are the maid of honor and Raegan is the matron of honor—and Vikki is the flower girl. She is *really* excited about being part of this wedding. When Matt and I asked her to be flower girl, she told me she wasn't able to take part in her mother's first wedding and she is very happy to be able to be part of this one—which I think is adorable."

"You didn't tell her that there wasn't a wedding, right?" Roe asked her sister. "She's a little young to take all that in."

"Vikki is a lot older than the date on her birth certificate claims," Riley answered loftily. "But Matt and I thought we'd save that little tidbit of information for another time just in case after hearing that, Vikki comes up with questions that wind up stumping us."

"Wise decision. What time do you want me at the church since I missed the original run-through?" Roe asked, referring to the original rehearsal.

"Father Lawrence gave me a list of possible times. Barring an emergency, how does three o'clock this afternoon sound to you?" Riley asked. "Whatever you pick, I'll call the others and tell them. Nobody else has any conflicts. I already checked."

"Three o'clock is doable—barring an emergency," Roe echoed her sister's words, although it would have to be a really big emergency to prevent her from getting there.

"Then I'll see you at the church at three o'clock—barring an emergency," both women said simultaneously, their voices blending. The conversation ended with a laugh. "Bye, Roe," Riley said just before she hung up.

Roe hit the "red" button to end the call. She listened to make sure the call was over, then sighed as she roused herself.

She didn't have time to stare off into oblivion. She had things to do. Not to mention a cattle herd to check out before she could show up at the local church for rehearsal.

There had been an anthrax scare far up north but with any luck, it was either a false alarm or a scare that wasn't going to work its way down to the area surrounding Forever. She had no idea how the local ranchers would respond to that sort of threat if it actually did materialize.

She fervently hoped she would never have to find out. She was perfectly happy to go through life without ever finding out if she was up to that sort of a large-scale challenge. She thought she was, but she would rather not have her abilities tested. Roe honestly felt she was perfectly fine handling mundane things and remaining unchallenged for the entire course of her career.

Dressed in jeans and a work shirt, as well as a denim jacket, and almost ready to leave, Roe came out into the small living room where Kingston was entertaining himself by chasing Lucy around.

"Try not to destroy the house while I'm gone, guys," she told her pets. "I'll try to get home at a decent hour, but I can't really promise anything. Barring any emergency and if the wedding rehearsal goes off on schedule, I'll be able to feed you on time—but don't hold me to that," she said, addressing her words to the lively, fluffy white dog that was busy spinning around in a wide circle in front of her.

She knew it was Kingston's way of trying to entertain her and getting her to stay.

Kingston made a noise, and it was almost as if he actually understood what she was saying to him.

Roe laughed as she petted one dog and then the other. "Glad we understand one another. I will see you two guys later—and remember, you're supposed to guard the house," she instructed.

Not that there was actually anything to guard against, she thought as she locked the door behind her. Forever, Texas, was part of a dying breed: a small, friendly town where everyone knew almost everyone else and looked out for one another to make sure that nothing happened. It was the very definition of the word "neighborly."

There were some exceptions, of course. After all, this was reality and that meant there were people who preferred to keep to themselves and avoid any sort of unnecessary interaction with anyone. But by and large, those people were mercifully few and far between.

For the most part, everyone in the small town knew everyone else and had known them for a very long time. The ones who hadn't been born in Forever had made a strong effort to become part of the town and blend in, often more than those who had been born here.

Roe checked her watch to see how much time she had before she needed to get to the church. Not showing up once was forgivable. Not showing up twice was another story entirely. And besides which, she did want to take part in this. After all, this was for Riley's wedding and she knew how important this was to all parties concerned.

Pacing herself, she paid visits to several of the local ranches to check on how their cattle were doing. Other than a couple of instances—in one case a calf had gotten tangled up in a section of barbed wire and it took a great deal of careful maneuvering to get the animal's horns uncoupled from the fencing—Roe's visits to the ranches were rather uneventful.

She would have never actually admitted it to anyone except for possibly her grandfather, but it was the wedding rehearsal that had captured the major part of her attention.

Because the last ranch on her list was farther away than the other two, it took her a while to get there. Consequently, the trip back took even longer, despite the fact that she hurried and drove her truck faster than normal. It turned out that she was the last one to arrive at the church anyway.

Riley was looking out the church window and was the first to see her coming.

When the front door opened, she greeted Roe, her brown-haired, brown-eyed mirror image with, "Ah, you're finally here. I was just about to send out the search party to look for you."

"Now you won't have to 'cause she's here," Vikki declared happily, a grin encompassing the red-haired little girl's small, beaming face.

"Yes, I am." Roe made her way over to Vikki. "Hi,

Angel. How are you doing?" she asked the little girl who was about to officially become part of their family once Riley married Vikki's father, Matt.

"I'm doing fine," the almost five-year-old answered solemnly, as if the question that had been put to her required deep thought. "How are you doing?" Vikki asked, turning the question back on Roe and looking very proud of herself for the accomplishment.

Roe struggled to keep from laughing out loud, knowing it would probably hurt Vikki's feelings. Her exchanges with the little girl always tickled her. She was rather amazed at how well Vikki had learned to cope with her mother's passing.

"I'm doing just fine, now that I see you here," Roe answered.

Her small, smooth brow furrowed as she tried to understand what Roe was saying to her. "You didn't think I would be here?" Vikki asked.

"Oh, but I did. After all, you're the flower girl. I just meant that I was really very happy to see you," Roe explained.

"Oh." Vikki's freshly arranged red hair bobbed up and down as she nodded. "Well, I'm happy to see you, too," she told Roe. "How's Kingston? You didn't bring him with you, did you?"

As she asked, the little girl quickly looked around the church in all the places that the dog would choose to hide.

"No, not this time, honey. He's home keeping Lucy company," Roe told Vikki, thinking that was the most understandable explanation she could tell her. "Lucy gets lonely whenever I leave the house."

Vikki thought that over for a minute. "Maybe I could go over to your house and keep her company."

"That's a lovely idea," Roe agreed, but then quickly added, "We'll see. Right now, they need you here for the ceremony."

"Oh, yeah," Vikki agreed, her expression looking almost solemn.

Father Lawrence chose that moment to walk out from his office and into the church proper. He clapped his hands together as he scanned the small gathering before him. It was composed of just the wedding party, not any of the guests.

"Well, it looks like everyone who is supposed to be here is here now," the tall, fair-haired, blue-eyed priest noted. "Shall we get started? Spoiler alert," he said, as if it was meant to be a side comment. "There are no surprises. This is going to be just like the last ceremony I officiated for you, except that it was for Raegan and Alan," he said with a wink. "This time it'll be for Riley and Matthew."

"And me!" Vikki piped up, excited.

Matt laughed and looked in wonder at the daughter he hadn't even known existed such a short while ago. Now her existence filled his heart in ways he couldn't have even begun to imagine. It wasn't until Riley, Breena's best friend, had written a letter telling him about Vikki. He had come to Forever not really knowing what to expect. He certainly hadn't expected to fall in love twice over.

But he had.

"Most definitely you, buttercup," Matt teased, giving the little girl an affectionate hug.

"I'm not a buttercup," Vikki said, pretending to protest. "I'm a girl."

"Yes, you most definitely are that," Matt agreed. Then he flushed and looked toward the priest, thinking the man was waiting to get started and he was interrupting. "Sorry, Father."

"No need to apologize." Father Lawrence nodded toward the little girl. "I find this sort of display very heartening. But, in deference to those here who are on a tighter schedule and would like to get things moving along, I do suggest we get started." Father Lawrence looked around the immediate area. "Any objections?"

Mike Robertson laughed and shook his head. "Not from this crowd, Father," he told the priest.

"All right, then let's begin—I promise this will be fast and painless, especially since we've already gone through it once before," the priest said as he smiled at the people standing around hm.

Vikki frowned as she tried to follow what the priest had just said. "No, we didn't," she protested.

"Father Lawrence is talking about when he married your aunt Raegan and your uncle Alan," Roe told Vikki, whispering into the little girl's ear.

Vikki's face lit up as comprehension suddenly filled her. "Oh, now I understand," she said. "Sorry, Father Lawrence."

Vikki didn't understand why everyone in the church

was suddenly laughing at what she had just said, but she politely refrained from asking because Father Lawrence seemed to want to move things along.

## Chapter Two

Mercifully, Father Lawrence had everyone go through their paces just once. When the wedding rehearsal finally ended, he smiled and said, "Well, that should do it. Nothing left to do, folks, but have the actual wedding take place," he told the small collection of people, his eyes washing over them.

"Can't we do it again, Father?" Vikki asked, her small voice echoing around the church and challenging the growing silence.

Surprised, Matt looked at his daughter. Kids her age liked to be outside and playing, not stuck indoors and being quiet.

"Why would you want to do it again?" he asked. He would have thought she would be bored by now. For all intents and purposes, she had behaved perfectly and been exceptionally quiet.

Vikki answered the question solemnly, her expression looking like the last word in sincerity.

"'Cause I want to make sure that I do it right. It's important to get it right, isn't it?" she asked, looking from Riley to her father. "This is your wedding and weddings are important," she stressed.

Matt didn't even try not to laugh. Getting down on one knee, he put his arms around the petite little girl and pulled her closer to him. He couldn't believe how lucky he was to have discovered he had a daughter after all this time and that she had turned out to be such a little darling. "Just having you here for the rehearsal is doing it right, sweetheart," he told her.

The puzzled look on Vikki's face testified to the fact that she really didn't understand, but she was not about to question such things in a room full of grown-ups. It was obvious she thought they might laugh at her.

Instead, she merely agreed with what her father had said. "Okay."

That was the moment that Miss Joan, the owner of the town's only diner, chose to breeze into the church. It was apparent by her intense expression that she had timed her entrance.

"Hello, Father," she said, greeting the man she'd known ever since he was a small boy. "All done here?" It was obvious that she thought he was and that she was asking what amounted to a rhetorical question.

"Hello, Miss Joan. Yes, we're all done here," Father Lawrence replied with a wide smile, then decided to compliment the woman. "You timed your entrance quite well, Miss Joan."

She didn't bother denying it. "I do my best," she replied. There was no missing the fact that she was quite pleased with herself. Her hazel eyes swept over the small gathering and she nodded. She saw what she needed to.

"Everyone hungry?" She wasn't expecting anyone to say "No."

"Because if you are," she went on, "there's a wedding rehearsal dinner waiting for all of you at the diner. Just follow your noses." Miss Joan looked amused as she waved her thin hand toward the church's double doors.

The way she worded her invitation, as well as her tone of voice, indicated that not only was everyone welcome to come to the diner, they were actually required to come there. Miss Joan was not accustomed to being turned down or having her invitation ignored, and to everyone's recollection, she really never had been.

Miss Joan was about to turn and walk out of the church when Vikki urgently tugged on the hem of the diner owner's dress. Hazel eyes looked down, pinning the little girl in place.

"Yes?" Miss Joan asked in the same voice she used whenever an adult wanted her attention.

"Will there be ice cream there?" Vikki asked her hopefully.

Miss Joan's expression never changed. "After you eat your dinner, yes, there will be ice cream there."

But Vikki wasn't finished asking questions. "Lots and lots of ice cream?" she asked.

Miss Joan treated the question as if it was actually a serious inquiry. "How much you eat is all up to your father," she told the little girl. And then she fixed Vikki with a look that had been known to make grown men flinch. "But a word to the wise, nobody wants to see you exploding, little girl."

The little girl giggled. "I wouldn't do that," she said, waving away the very idea. "People don't explode if they eat too much.

"Well, I certainly hope not," Miss Joan said. "But you never know. Just remember, if you do explode, then you're going to have to be the one who cleans everything all up." She looked down at Vikki pointedly. "Understand?"

Her eyes met Miss Joan's, and she nodded her head up and down so hard, her red hair bobbed almost frantically now.

"I understand," the little girl echoed in a serious tone.

For one of the few times in her life, Miss Joan actually found herself struggling to keep the corners of her mouth from curving upward. There was no doubt about it, the woman got a huge kick out of the little girl, far more of a kick than she had gotten out of a child in years.

Against all odds, she succeeded in keeping any hint of the smile from her face. Only then did she speak, declaring a single word, "Good," and accompanying the single word with a nod of her head. And then, for good measure, she looked around the small gathering. "All right, everyone, get in your vehicles and come on down to the diner," she instructed.

With that, Miss Joan turned on her stacked heel and walked out of the church.

With a laugh, Roe looked in Matt's direction. "You

know," she commented, "I think Miss Joan had to have been a general in her previous life."

Absorbing every word that was being said around her, Vikki's mouth dropped open in total awe. "Really?" she cried, her eyes huge. She looked from Roe to her father, as well as at several other faces. The little girl appeared to be utterly captivated by this newest piece of news.

Riley made no effort to keep from laughing. "I think your aunt Roe is teasing you," she told the little girl.

Hearing the comment, Vikki shook her head. "She's not my aunt yet. She won't be my aunt until after the wedding."

Amazed, Matt was beginning to think that it was going to take the combined efforts of all the adults gathered together in the church at this very moment to stay one crucial step ahead of his bright little girl.

"You're absolutely right," he told his daughter. "Tell me, how did you ever get to be so very smart?"

Vikki never even blinked. "I was born that way," she informed him proudly. "Mama said so."

Riley tilted her head slightly, trying to keep the tears from falling from her eyes. Breena would have been so proud of Vikki. Riley could swear she could hear her late best friend's voice talking to the little girl, patiently teaching her things. Breena never talked to Vikki as if she was a child, treating her instead like an adult waiting to happen.

Turning to look at her, Matt thought he saw the glimmer of tears in Riley's eyes. "Are you all right?" he whispered to the woman he was going to make his wife.

Recovering, Riley got hold of herself and flashed a smile at Matt as she took Vikki's hand in hers. "I'm just fine, Matt."

Roe looked on, feeling more than a little envious. She dearly loved both of her sisters and was very happy that Raegan had found someone to love and that Riley had as well, but there was a part of her that was envious of the fact that both of her sisters had found what amounted to their "other halves" while she felt unattached and in all probability would continue to feel that way for possibly the rest of her life.

Oh well, Roe thought philosophically, she had signed on to do her very best to take care of the animals who came her way and that was turning out very well. That was what she needed to focus on, not on what she didn't have.

She got into her own vehicle at the same time that everyone else was getting into theirs. Roe decided to turn on some music to drown out any sad, interfering thoughts that might wind up distracting her. She turned the volume up high and drove herself over to Miss Joan's diner.

Miss Joan wanted this to be a pre-celebratory party, and Roe wasn't going to allow any sober thoughts to get in her way and bring her down.

This was definitely not the time to feel sorry for herself, Roe silently lectured.

This was about Riley and Matt and the sweet little girl who was officially going to become part of their family once Riley and Matt said "I do." Anything she could do to help that happen was absolutely perfect in her book.

* * *

When Roe arrived at Miss Joan's diner, she half expected to see a notice on the door declaring that the diner was closed for a private party. But there was no such notice. Miss Joan was apparently juggling both the rehearsal dinner and her regular customers with both hands. She had a section cordoned off so the wedding party, along with Father Lawrence, who had been included in the invitation, were able to sit together while Miss Joan's regulars still had tables available for coffee and their meals as usual.

Vikki gleefully found herself smack dab in the center of the wedding party's seating arrangement. It was obvious to anyone who looked that the little girl loved being the center of attention. She talked up a storm. Riley and her entire family loved Vikki dearly.

"Smile, Roe," Raegan ordered her sister as she came up to join her. "Otherwise, those furrows in your brow are going to be permanent."

Roe had no idea she had been frowning. She flushed. Then, instead of making up excuses about why she looked that way, Roe told her sister honestly, "I'm just worried."

"Well, that certainly narrows things down," Riley said flippantly. "Look, we just came through a history-changing drought and managed to survive just fine, thanks to some of the precautions that our team made. Everything else just naturally winds up taking second place," Raegan assured her.

Roe knew that Raegan knew what she was talking about. Raegan and her husband, along with several of the men he had brought into the project, were responsible for saving Forever from suffering a really terrible fate, possibly a permanent one. They had managed to build a reservoir and also drill for water, bringing it to the all-but-dried-out area and eventually reviving it.

"Not everything," Roe murmured almost to herself.

Raegan was immediately alert. "Would you care to elaborate?"

Roe realized that her sister had heard her. She most definitely didn't want to elaborate. "I don't want to get ahead of myself," Roe told Raegan.

"Oh no, you don't get to toss out unnerving statements and then retreat as if you hadn't said anything at all. Now out with it, Roe. Is there something we should all be bracing for?" Raegan asked.

Before Roe had a chance to come up with an acceptable answer, Riley leaned over and got into the discussion. "What are we talking about and why does my matron of honor look as if she's just bitten into a sour piece of fruit?"

Roe decided to quickly wave away the question. "Nothing to concern yourself about," she told her sister firmly, flashing a smile at Riley. "I told you, all you're supposed to be focused on is your bridegroom, your adorable imp of a daughter, and the upcoming wedding. Everything else is just everything else."

"You know, I'd really feel a lot better about it if you weren't such a terrible liar," Riley told Roe.

"I'm not lying," Roe told her, trying to look like the absolute soul of innocence. "What I am is exhausted," she emphasized. "I got about twelve minutes of sleep last night and just when I was finally drifting off, I was awakened by two madly moving little tongues washing my cheeks and doing their very best to wake me up. Apparently, they thought it was time for breakfast."

Riley looked at Raegan dubiously. "Do you believe her?" she asked the first triplet to exchange marriage vows.

"I'm not all that sure if we have much of a choice. Our sister can be pretty closemouthed when she wants to be," Raegan complained.

Roe had had enough. "Stop interrogating me. This is supposed to be a party," she reminded her sisters. "If you're not careful, Miss Joan is going to come over and start asking questions. And you *know* she's not going to retreat until she's satisfied that she managed to get the truth out of us."

Riley looked up as a shadow was suddenly cast over her. "Speak of the devil," Riley murmured under her breath.

"You're not calling me the devil, are you?" Miss Joan asked Riley, coming up behind the two young women and putting an arm around each one of them with just enough pressure exerted to make them realize she had overheard them.

"Oh no, we wouldn't dream of doing that, Miss Joan. Everyone knows you're the very opposite of the devil," Riley told her solemnly.

Miss Joan gave the bride-to-be a very penetrating look. "You're just afraid that I'm going to make you wash all the dishes on this table once everyone is done eating," the woman quipped.

"I can wash them for you," Vikki piped up, happily volunteering her services. The little girl bobbed her head up and down in assurance as she added, "Mama taught me how."

This time Miss Joan actually did laugh out loud, tickled. "I'll keep you in mind if my dishwasher breaks."

Vikki obviously thought that Miss Joan was talking about a person, not a machine. "Do people break?" she asked, wide-eyed.

"Not usually, little one," Riley told Matt's daughter. She pointed to Vikki's dinner plate. "Eat up so you can have dessert," she coaxed.

Picking up her fork, Vikki did as she was told, applying herself diligently to the contents of her plate and quickly making what was on it disappear.

Before she made her way over to the other guests seated in the diner, Miss Joan paused to bend toward Roe. "Before you leave my establishment, I'd like a word with you, missy," she told her.

Roe felt her stomach tightening. This sounded serious. "About?" she asked Miss Joan, the word all but sticking in her throat.

"You'll find out when the time comes and I tell you, won't you?" Miss Joan asked Roe cheerfully. With that, she turned on her heel and made her way to the other guests at the table and then, to the ones in the diner.

Roe sat and watched the woman go. She was afraid to hazard a guess as to what Miss Joan wanted to talk to her about.

## Chapter Three

As it turned out, Roe was destined to wait until everyone included in the wedding party finally walked out of the diner before Miss Joan turned her attention to her.

Coming her way, Miss Joan frowned as she looked at Riley's maid of honor.

"You know, you look like you're waiting for the executioner to come your way and throw the fatal switch, electrocuting you," the diner owner commented. Her eyes met Roe's. "I'm not as scary as all that, am I, girl?"

There was no point in trying to bluff her way through this or denying what the woman had just said, Roe thought. And there was certainly no point in lying to her. Miss Joan had a way of seeing through everything.

Roe's eyes met Miss Joan's. Very briefly, she thought of denying it, and then she admitted, "Sometimes."

Contrary to what she expected, Roe's answer seemed

to amuse the woman. Miss Joan allowed a glimmer of a smile to pass over her lips before she finally told Roe why she wanted to see her. "Well, honey, the reason I called you over is because, quite frankly, I was worried about you."

"You were worried about me? Why?" Roe asked, confused. Why would Miss Joan even say something like that? She had absolutely no idea where this was going.

"Yes." Miss Joan circled around to where Roe was seated, looking at her critically. "You look like death warmed over, girl." The diner owner studied her more closely, as if she expected to see the answer to her question in Roe's eyes. "You getting enough sleep?"

The answer was no, but she wasn't about to admit that to the owner of the diner. Instead, Roe gave the woman an indirect answer. "I plan to get some tonight. I'm going straight home from here, feeding the dogs and then crawling into bed." She waited to see if that satisfied the woman.

Miss Joan looked knowingly at the girl she had helped bring into the world. "It might help you get that extra sleep you need if you remembered to close your bedroom door at night."

Roe read between the lines. She had no idea how Miss Joan had guessed that her dogs were responsible for waking her up way too early in the morning. But she had made her peace with the same fact as everyone else did. This was Miss Joan and that meant somehow, the woman always seemed to know everything.

So rather than protest, or agree to the idea that she

was going to lock her pets out, Roe merely just agreed. "Sounds like a good idea."

Miss Joan snorted as she looked at the vet knowingly. "But you don't plan on doing it, do you? You do know those dogs aren't going to get insulted if you bar them from your bedroom, especially for your own survival." And then the diner owner shrugged, her thin shoulders moving up and down. "But you do what you feel is best."

Finished with her commentary, Miss Joan leveled a piercing gaze at her. "Now go home, girl," she ordered. "I don't want to hear about you falling asleep behind the wheel of your truck and landing in some ditch when I get up tomorrow morning."

"Yes, ma'am," Roe agreed contritely. She gathered her things together and got up from her seat.

The thing about Miss Joan was that beneath all that surface bluster, she knew the woman actually cared. And that, in the long run, was all that really mattered.

Roe didn't quite remember the drive back to her home, but not for the first time, she was really grateful that she lived in town and not on her grandfather's ranch the way she and her sisters had for all those years growing up. The way she felt right now, Roe knew she might have been in real danger of actually falling asleep behind the wheel the way that Miss Joan worried she might.

Falling into a ditch was another matter, though. There weren't all that many ditches to fall into in and around Forever.

She congratulated herself when she pulled up in front of her house.

The moment Roe unlocked her front door, she was immediately greeted by almost nonstop barking. The dogs, she had long ago concluded, were expressing their joy at having her come home. Kingston was racing around her, creating a fluffy white circle until Roe finally bent down to slow him down and run her hand over his fur to pet him.

As if sensing what was going on, Lucy gave the smaller dog a moment to bond with his mistress, then nosed the little guy out of the way so she could have her turn with her mistress as well.

"Yes, yes, I missed you guys, too," Roe laughed despite herself. As she petted each dog, she said, "But you have to promise to be good tonight." She rose then and went into the kitchen.

Opening the refrigerator, she began preparing food for Kingston's and Lucy's evening meal. "I'm going to feed you and then I'm going to bed," she informed the dogs, talking to them as if they were absorbing her every word. "Thanks to you guys and your morning alarm system, Miss Joan commented on the fact that I look like I am dead on my feet." She frowned and shook her head. "You can imagine how well that went over."

Their barking grew louder, as if they were expressing their opinion on that.

Roe placed servings of chicken, a sprinkling of cheese and the all-important spoonful of ground pumpkin in each bowl, then brought the bowls over to their feeding spot.

She was convinced that Kingston was going to sprain a least one paw if not two by dancing around her, salivating madly.

"Miss Joan said I should lock you guys out of my bedroom if I want any peace and quiet, but I'm not going to do that—if you two promise to behave yourselves and be good. Do you?" Roe asked, eyeing her two pets as if she expected an answer from them. She placed the bowls of food on the floor. She turned and went to fill up their water bowls.

The dogs lost no time in scarfing up their dinner. Roe had a feeling that, left to their own devices, the dogs would go on eating until they wound up exploding. She was going to need to keep an eye on them, she decided. She definitely didn't want them overeating.

But that was something she would look into tomorrow, she told herself. Tonight was meant for sleeping— which she was going to do immediately.

Roe fell asleep the moment her head hit the pillow. So fast, in fact, that she didn't even notice the blinking light on her answering machine.

The following morning for once, she woke up herself, without the dogs anointing her cheeks in an effort to rouse her from sleep. She had slept later than usual and felt both grateful and a little bit guilty for leaving the dogs to their own devices like this—but mainly she felt grateful.

She stretched, feeling like an entirely new person from the one she had been yesterday morning. She walked over to the door and opened it, then quickly got back into her bed a hair's breadth ahead of the dogs.

Sitting up, she patted the place beside her and was instantly rewarded with not one but two dogs bounding over to sit on either side of her.

Their expressions all but said, "Weren't we good? Aren't you proud of us?"

Roe laughed. "Thanks, guys," she told them. "I really needed that sleep. To show you how grateful I am, I'm going to get your breakfast and put it out *before* I take my shower this morning."

As Roe walked into the kitchen, she saw the landline blinking. Whether it had been doing that last night or someone had called earlier yesterday, she had no way of knowing. She was going to need to hit the "play" button to find out.

But that was for after she prepared breakfast for the dogs. She quickly did a repeat of last night's meal, then set both bowls down on the floor.

"Eat up, boys and girls. Today feels like it's going to be another busy, long day. I've got several appointments coming into my office, not to mention a maid of honor dress to pick up. You wouldn't know about being a maid of honor, would you?" she asked with a laugh as the dogs paused to cock their heads at her, as if they were waiting for her to elaborate. "Trust me, it's a big deal in the human world," she told them. "Anyway, I'll probably be late coming home tonight so I'll leave you a lot of water to tie you over until I can get back."

Finished with the dogs, Roe stretched and yawned, then went back into the bedroom. She was going to postpone finding out who had left the message on her landline until after she had taken her shower.

But as usual, her curiosity got the better of her.

Hopefully, whatever it was could be quickly handled with a "yes" or "no" answer, she thought. Those were few and far between, but they did exist on occasion, Roe told herself, crossing her fingers.

She pressed the "play" button as she held the receiver to her ear.

Roe knew that her friends had far more sophisticated devices when it came to communication, but she tended to gravitate toward more old-fashioned things. She liked those better. There were times when she felt that the world was moving much too fast for her.

"Dr. Robertson," the deep voice on the other end of the call began, "This is Christopher Parnell. I don't know if you remember me or not, but I think I might need your help."

Remember him? Roe thought, amused by his choice of words. She might not have spoken to him for a number of years, but she certainly remembered him. She vividly remembered him from a time when there was no need to refer to her as "Dr. Robertson."

They had gone to school together, with Chris being a couple years ahead of her. At the time, she had had a giant-sized crush on him.

Actually, if she thought about it, Roe mused, a part of her still did, more or less. More than less, she amended. The very thought of seeing him had her blood rushing rather madly through her veins in anticipation.

She could remember watching him in a rodeo competition one summer. The competition involved his coming in first riding his palomino, Big Jake. He had also taken third place in a bronco-busting event, which she had found even more impressive. Roe could recall him looking absolutely magnificent on the back of that horse, hanging on tightly as the horse did his best to buck him off.

But then Chris had graduated high school and, with everything she had been involved in, Roe had lost track of him. She did remember hearing that he had applied to college and was accepted and she had thought that was that. But the following spring, his father had died. The question of who would take care of the ranch came up, but his older brother, Pete, didn't want to be bothered with it. Pete had other plans for himself. He just wanted to sell his share.

Chris didn't want to see the ranch falling into the wrong hands, or actually into any other hands, so he had scraped together as much money as he could and bought his brother out. What he wasn't able to come up with, he borrowed and made arrangements to make regular payments on the property, which he did, although it wasn't easy, until it finally became his free and clear.

She knew all this and admired it. She admired other things about Chris as well, she thought, smiling to herself.

Roe listened to the rest of the message on the machine. The Chris Parnell she recalled from high school had been a happy, fun-loving guy. The voice on her answering machine sounded as if all the fun had been summarily drained out of him.

All he had said was he thought he might have a problem, adding that he never thought he would ever wind up calling her for help. Yet, that was exactly what he was now doing.

He left his number and asked her to call him back at the first chance she had.

Roe really wished she had seen his message earlier, but there was no going back to rectify that error, she thought. All she could do was move forward and do things in the present.

She replayed the message, listening more closely and jotting down his phone number. Roe planned on calling Chris the moment she finished showering and getting dressed.

Fifteen minutes later, she was dried off and dressed and dialing the number she had jotted down.

Instead of getting him, she found she was listening to a recording.

"This is Chris Parnell. I can't answer my phone right now. Leave me your name, your number and a message and I'll get back to you as soon as I can. I'll be branding my cattle in the north forty, so it might be a while before I can get back to you."

The call abruptly ended.

Roe frowned at the receiver in her hand. She really didn't have time to play phone tag, she thought, hanging up the landline receiver. She supposed she could try calling him again later, but this "phone tag" could very well go on indefinitely, and there was something in his voice that made her think he was really worried. She wondered if there was a problem with his cattle.

She remembered him as a far more upbeat guy and not a worrier. Things had obviously changed.

She caught the bottom of her lip between her teeth, and worked it, thinking. He said he was going to be branding cattle in the north forty. She was basically familiar with where that was on his property.

Never one to put things off, Roe decided she could easily ride over to his ranch to see him and get to the bottom of whatever was bothering him. She had to admit that her curiosity was definitely aroused.

Grateful that there was no wedding rehearsal scheduled for today, Roe finished getting dressed. She pulled on her boots and took off the moment she was ready. She made a mental note on the way over, to call the animal owners who had appointments in her office today and push those appointments up by an hour or so, citing a medical emergency that required her attention.

She smiled to herself. It occurred to her that the people of Forever were basically a very understanding lot. Thank goodness for that.

*Don't miss*
Matchmaker on the Ranch *by Marie Ferrarella,*
*available August 2023 wherever*
*Harlequin® Special Edition*
*books and ebooks are sold.*

*www.Harlequin.com*

### #3001 THE MAVERICK'S SWEETEST CHOICE
*Montana Mavericks: Lassoing Love* • by Stella Bagwell
Rancher Dale Dalton only planned to buy cupcakes from the local bakery. Yet one look at single mom Kendra Humphrey and it's love at first sight. Or at least lust. Kendra wants more than a footloose playboy for her and her young daughter. But Dale's full-charm offensive may be too tempting and delicious to ignore!

### #3002 FAKING A FAIRY TALE
*Love, Unveiled* • by Teri Wilson
Bridal editor Daphne Ballantyne despises her coworker Jack King. But when a juicy magazine assignment requires going undercover as a blissfully engaged couple, both Daphne and Jack say "I do." If only their intense marriage charade wasn't beginning to feel a lot like love...

### #3003 HOME FOR THE CHALLAH DAYS
by Jennifer Wilck
Sarah Abrams is home for Rosh Hashanah...but can't be in the same room as her ex-boyfriend. She broke Aaron Isaacson's heart years ago and he's still deeply hurt. Until targeted acts of vandalism bring the reluctant duo together. And unearth buried—and undeniable—attraction just in time for the holiday.

### #3004 A CHARMING DOORSTEP BABY
*Charming, Texas* • by Heatherly Bell
Dean Hunter's broken childhood still haunts him. So there's no way the retired rodeo star will let his neighbor Maribel Del Toro call social services on a mother who suddenly left her daughter in Maribel's care. They'll *both* care for the baby...and maybe even each other.

### #3005 HER OUTBACK RANCHER
*The Brands of Montana* • by Joanna Sims
Hawk Bowhill's heart is on his family's cattle ranch in Australia. But falling for fiery Montana cowgirl Jessie Brand leads to a bevy of challenges, and geography is the least of them. From two continents to her unexpected pregnancy to her family's vow to keep them apart, will the price of happily-ever-after be too high to pay?

### #3006 HIS UNLIKELY HOMECOMING
*Small-Town Sweethearts* • by Carrie Nichols
Shop owner Libby Taylor isn't fooled by Nick Cabot's tough motorcycle-riding exterior. He helped her daughter find her lost puppy...and melted Libby's guarded emotions in the process. But despite Nick's tender, heroic heart, can she take a chance on love with a man convinced he's unworthy of it?

# Get 3 FREE REWARDS!

**We'll send you 2 FREE Books plus a FREE Mystery Gift.**

**FREE** Value Over **$20**

Both the **Harlequin® Special Edition** and **Harlequin® Heartwarming™** series feature compelling novels filled with stories of love and strength where the bonds of friendship, family and community unite.

---

**YES!** Please send me 2 FREE novels from the Harlequin Special Edition or Harlequin Heartwarming series and my FREE Gift (gift is worth about $10 retail). After receiving them, if I don't wish to receive any more books, I can return the shipping statement marked "cancel." If I don't cancel, I will receive 6 brand-new Harlequin Special Edition books every month and be billed just $5.49 each in the U.S. or $6.24 each in Canada, a savings of at least 12% off the cover price, or 4 brand-new Harlequin Heartwarming Larger-Print books every month and be billed just $6.24 each in the U.S. or $6.74 each in Canada, a savings of at least 19% off the cover price. It's quite a bargain! Shipping and handling is just 50¢ per book in the U.S. and $1.25 per book in Canada.* I understand that accepting the 2 free books and gift places me under no obligation to buy anything. I can always return a shipment and cancel at any time by calling the number below. The free books and gift are mine to keep no matter what I decide.

Choose one:  ☐ **Harlequin Special Edition** (235/335 BPA GRMK)   ☐ **Harlequin Heartwarming Larger-Print** (161/361 BPA GRMK)   ☐ **Or Try Both!** (235/335 & 161/361 BPA GRPZ)

Name (please print)

Address _____ Apt. #

City _____ State/Province _____ Zip/Postal Code

**Email:** Please check this box ☐ if you would like to receive newsletters and promotional emails from Harlequin Enterprises ULC and its affiliates. You can unsubscribe anytime.

### Mail to the **Harlequin Reader Service:**
**IN U.S.A.:** P.O. Box 1341, Buffalo, NY 14240-8531
**IN CANADA:** P.O. Box 603, Fort Erie, Ontario L2A 5X3

Want to try 2 free books from another series! Call 1-800-873-8635 or visit www.ReaderService.com.

---

HSEHW23

# HARLEQUIN
## PLUS

Try the best multimedia subscription service for romance readers like you!

---

## Read, Watch and Play.

Experience the easiest way to get the romance content you crave.

Start your **FREE TRIAL** at
<u>www.harlequinplus.com/freetrial</u>.